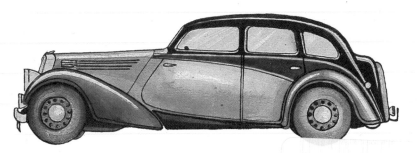

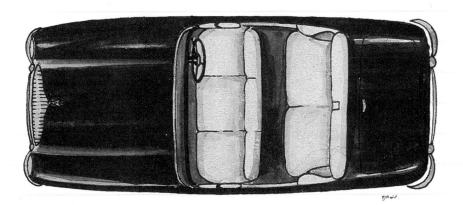

FLYING STANDARD

FLYWHEEL

"Keeps the Works Going Round on the Idle Strokes"

Production

- STUBBS -

FLYWHEEL

MEMORIES·OF
THE·OPEN·ROAD

TOM SWALLOW ARTHUR H PILL
President   Chairman
AND THE MEMBERS OF THE MUHLBERG MOTOR CLUB
STALAG IVB · GERMANY · 1944 – 1945

Webb & Bower
MICHAEL JOSEPH

Front endpaper illustration – The Ideal Car (British)
Back endpaper illustration – The Ideal Car (American)

FLYWHEEL Supplement – The Ideal Car page 239

First published in Great Britain 1987 by
Webb & Bower (Publishers) Limited
9 Colleton Crescent, Exeter, EX2 4BY
in association with
Michael Joseph Limited
27 Wright's Lane, London W8 5SL

Designed and produced by Facer Publishing
7 Colleton Crescent, Exeter EX2 4DG, England

**British Library Cataloguing in
Publication Data**

Flywheel: memories of the open road from
Stalag IVB Germany 1944/45.
I. World War, 1939–45—Prisoners and
prisons, German
I. Swallow, Tom
940.54′72′43   D805.G3

ISBN 0–86350–151–6

Typeset by P&M Typesetting, Exeter

Colour origination by Peninsular Repro
Services, Exeter

Printed and bound in Great Britain by Purnell
Book Production Limited, Paulton, Bristol

CONTENTS

INTRODUCTION

Stalag IVB was situated near Muhlberg-on-Elbe, a small inland port in what is now East Germany, some 80 miles south of Berlin and close to Torgau, the meeting place of the converging American and Russian Armies. *Stalag* is an abbreviation of the German word *Stammlager* which means *basecamp*. There were hundreds of them in Germany. 'IVB' was designed to hold about 15,000 prisoners but often held nearer 30,000 in the filthy, cold wooden huts which were infested with all kinds of vermin.

Living under such conditions, with nothing to do and nowhere to go, men died quite easily – often of a strange lethargy that seemed to take away their zest for life. In an attempt to raise the morale and spirit of the camp, all sorts of organisations were set up and one such was the 'Muhlberg Motor Club'. The MMC's aims were to bring motoring enthusiasts together, to find work for idle hands and minds and to educate the 'new motorists'.

It was an almost instant success and the membership grew rapidly from the six who attended the first meeting to about 200. At one committee meeting I suggested that the club should produce its own motoring magazine to keep its members abreast of the motoring times and to educate those members who had learnt to drive in the Armed Forces but who had never owned a vehicle.

We did not have to look far for staff. Every member of the committee 'volunteered' for the job. Pat Harrington-Johnson, a journalist back home in South Africa, was the obvious choice as Editor and I became his 'staff reporter'. Les 'Dai' Davis, a truck driver in civvy street, was appointed Diesel Expert and Maurice Airey took over as Sports Cars Expert ably assisted by Bill Trevvett who also doubled as artist. 'Club Runner' sounded a bit 'ordinary' so Alan Vidow was appointed Circulation Manager.

Chairman Arthur Pill took over as Production Manager. His was a daunting task and he performed miracles. There was nothing to write on and nothing to write with but by adopting a system of beg, borrow, buy or barter (stealing from Jerry was taken for granted), he slowly began to get his act together. Arthur begged a pen-holder, borrowed a nib, bought some ink with *Lagergeld* (camp money) and bartered cigarettes for something to write on. Someone liberated some quinine tablets from the German sick bay for colour but heaven knows how Arthur managed to acquire the millet soup which was our staple diet at the time. He must have gone short himself.

Millet soup it was discovered began to ferment after four or five days and became very gooey. It was used to stick things in the school exercise books that became the magazines and they are still 'stuck' after 43 years. Even today Arthur's 1944 Introduction to the first bound volume of *Flywheel* expresses quite clearly our pride and satisfaction in the production of our own magazine.

'Did I do that?' or 'Good God!' – these are but few of the expressions used by countless authors, playwrights and painters when reviewing some of their early work. In our own modest way we have expressed some such remarks – though possibly a trifle more to the point.

When, however, our founder and president – Tommy Swallow, first suggested a club magazine, well – it seemed a bit ambitious, to say the least of it. Nevertheless, the first issue took root and slowly emerged, thanks to S. E. ('Topper') Brown and Pat Harrington-Johnson.

Succeeding issues grew and blossomed out – amid many headaches and heartburns – those days when millet soup stuck down illustrations, the borrowed ink and pen nib, (we owned a holder) and – Oh! everything. Then the climb to the dizzy heights when we were offered the full time services of a commercial artist and a permanent script writer.

We think the succeeding issues are proof in themselves, so in finally publishing *Flywheel*, a British P.O.W. motoring magazine, we have purposely left the monthly publications as they were originally produced. – After all, man's progress is judged by the results.

It must now be recorded that without the wholehearted assistance of Messrs. Bill Stobbs, Tom Rodger, Bob Mumford and Alan Vidow, the development would not have been what it is today. Thanks are also offered to Messrs. Bill Trevvett and Maurice Airey for unstinted and expert advice; to Ray Newell for 'pictures', and 'Hari' Hopkins for his cartoons. Special mention must also be made of Roy Clacket for his excellent editiorial blocks.

Finally, if in a more salubrious residence you should once more scan these pages – just remember – the bangings, jolting, spilt 'brews', jam spots – rain spots and general misabuse that formed the immediate surroundings which gave birth to the *Flywheel*.

In 1945 he wrote a Foreword to the second bound volume of *Flywheel* which the production of this book has proved to be prophetic...

It still remains our intention to preserve the *Flywheel* volumes as they return from their period of hand circulation. The varying conditions of cleanliness will testify to the prevailing camp conditions. Later readers who, encosed in easy chairs and with a well stocked library to hand, may scoff to themselves in an all knowing way at what appears to be a glaring 'bloomer', are asked to remember that by far the greatest volume of material is taken from memory, and filtered through barbed wire at that.

However, read on. We passed our time pleasurably so perhaps you will excuse us if we remark that the opinion of the 'outside world' is secondary to us.

To Harrington-Johnson must go the credit for the name *The Flywheel*. Both the magazine and its mechanical namesake were designed to 'Keep the Works Going Round on the Idle Strokes'.

Every committeeman became a 'writer' – a temporary expert in his field – and after two months hard endeavour the first copy of *The Flywheel* appeared.

Flywheel No 1 was highly acclaimed and it and each succeeding edition was passed to club members by the Circulation Manager Alan Vidow, whose job it was to take each edition to every club member and collect it later. He had to find the bed spaces of up to 150 readers. The publication was an instant success and a wall supplement was produced for the benefit of the camp at large. This was pinned to a plywood board and 'loaned' to each hut for half a day – another job for Alan. The magazine, which was often read by members' friends, soon began to suffer from rough useage and one edition was badly damaged by a spilled cup of cocoa and had to be largely rewritten. A strong cover was made from hard cardboard covered with a kind of rexine. It was decorated with the Club's 'MMC' initials and a model motorcycle flywheel assembly. The badges were all cut out from an Italian aluminium mess-tin with the only tool available – a razor blade.

Bill Stobbs soon became our resident artist and was joined by Dudley Mumford and others who greatly improved the quality of the production but none more than Tom Rodger who took over the printing, painstakingly hand writing page after page, day after day – a full time job!

It was not very easy trying to hand script a magazine in a room occupied by about 200 other inmates each doing his own 'thing' such as making mugs and plates from empty tins, trying out newly-written songs on home-made instruments, rehearsing plays, shouting, singing, cursing and farting (the food was awful!).

On one never-to-be-forgotten occasion an empty barrack was found and the

Flywheel printers moved in post haste. They beat a hastier retreat when the floor began to move . . . towards them! Millions and millions of fleas!

I used my monthly letter allowance to contact Isle of Man TT winner Graham Walker, father of Murray and then editor of *Motor Cycling*, who was a great help and towards the end managed to get copies of 'Road Tests Recalled' sent out. These were bound between hard covers and formed part of the Club Library.

My Mum was an enthusiastic helper and sent cuttings from current magazines including second-hand prices and reports of wartime motoring events and thereby helped the Club to keep track of the outside world.

Flywheel No 11 was in production when the fighting reached Muhlberg and the camp was overrun by Cossacks of the First Ukrainian Army who, seeing that the sentry boxes were empty, mounted a guard and held us for a further six weeks or so, as hostages it was feared. Having eaten all the available food – potatoes – we were marched to Riesa and were later 'found' by the Americans who organised transport to move us out.

In the confusion that followed the end of the war, Arthur and I spent many months in hospital and by the time I had lost my colon and become a pioneer ileostomist, we were scattered to The Four Winds I had so often written about.

I kept in touch with old 'muckers' in Australia, Canada, Rhodesia, South Africa and the UK and am still making new contacts.

On a visit to see the Club Chairman in Canada in the mid 1970s, Arthur was able to report that most of the Club's treasures were safe. They were returned to the UK in 1985 in time for the 40th Anniversary of our liberation.

It gives me great pleasure, on behalf of all the members of The Muhlberg Motor Club, to donate the whole of my proceeds from this book to the British Red Cross Society in appreciation of their efforts on our behalf. Without them, The Order of St. John of Jerusalem and the Women's Voluntary Service (WVS), who packed our food parcels, many of us would not have survived.

Tom Swallow

At the end of the book there is a copy of one of our Wall Supplements *depicting our idea of the* **Ideal Car** *which was arrived at after many hundreds of man-hours of discussion. It is interesting to note that even in 1944 we envisaged that turbo-charging would be the most efficient method of boosting the power of an internal combustion engine. Today many cars proudly carry the 'turbo' badge but in 1944 this was definitely something for the future and gives some indication of the seriousness with which we approached our deliberations.*

The endpapers illustrate the British and American interpretation of our **Ideal Car.**

The FLYWHEEL

KEEPS THE WORKS GOING ROUND ON THE IDLE STROKES

15th. Sept. 1944.   Vol. I.   No 5.   Mühlberg - on - Elbe.

After the fuss the Ideal Car caused in camp (they are still arguing about it in some compounds) we thought it should be "the sensation of Earls Court." That presupposed a motor show, so- Anyway, it's time we had one... What with all these credits and rumours the blokes must see what they'll get for their money.

Perhaps it's a coincidence that this is our fifth issue - and it's five years since we had a motor show arranged (it wasn't held···)

If the models shown seem out of date — remember that they are the latest British productions (even if '39) and with the '42 U.S. stuff will probably be about what you will find in the first post- war exhibition. (Thanks to Allan Bowman and Bill Trevett for 'pikchers'.)

Now that the famous Quiz is over, we feel we must, (as one of them) pay a high tribute to the winning team's very fine — (censored- amid uproar by staff!.) Editor.

1944 MOTOR SHOW

Beauty of line and high performance combined with moderate price make the 2½ litre S.S. Jaguar saloon deservedly popular. Priced at £395 it has an overhead-valve 6 Cylinder engine of 20 h.p.

Jaguar

Priced at $860 the 1942 Chevrolet is a low priced American automobile. The L-head engine developes 90 b.h.p. and the body, mounted on a wheelbase of 118 ins. is said to possess the most graceful lines of any Chevrolet yet produced.

HILLMAN

One of England's most popular light cars, the 10h.p. Hillman Minx is shown here with a 2-door drop-head coupé body costing £215 in 1939.

Slightly higher in price than the low priced Buick, the 1941 model De Soto, which has a 6-cylinder engine developing 100 b.h.p, and a 123 inch wheelbase,- costs $ 940.

FLYING STANDARD

Distinctive body lines identify the 1939 Flying Standard '12' which has a 4-cylinder high-efficiency side-valve engine.

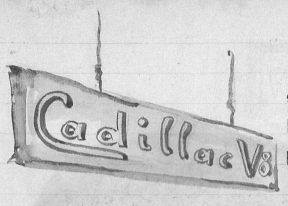

Cocktail bars and vanity sets are frequently found in the 7-passenger Cadillac on the 142 inch chassis. It has a V8 engine developing 160 b.h.p. Priced at $2,000 in 1941.

The 1941 Ford V8 5-passenger sedan bears close resemblance to previous models. It's well known side-valve engine gives 85 b.h.p. whilst the car retails at $850 in the U.S.A.

DELAHAYE

With the very successful 6-cylinder 3½-litre engine, the Delahaye which is shown here with typical French coachwork, has an outstanding performance. A V12 4½ litre, which has a racing tradition, is also made.

Fitted on a two-wheeled chassis this travelling home will accomodate four persons with comfort and provide sheer luxury for two.

Butane gas cooker and lighting, spring beds and close coupled four wheel suspension combined with pleasing appearance make this exhib outstanding.

An internal windscreen wiper, with automatic spring return. This gadget is fitted by suction pad to the windscreen.

Philips' "Duplolux", a select lamp incorporating a built in shock-breaker, carefully centred filament in a ribbed glass bulb giving a strong yellow light.

Dunlopillo

A boon for short statured drivers, these "Dunlopillo" cushions make seats adjustable in height and so increases driving comfort.

The events of the past few weeks would seem to indicate that in the not too distant future we shall be awheel once more and in a position to enjoy the fresh air of the home countryside; to speed along the main highways or to dawdle idly through the little lanes and byeways that we knew so well.

I am determined to break all rules and regulations by rising one morning early and rootling off to my favourite local beauty spots, Clent Hills, and climbing to the top on my machine, riding blissfully past the notice which says "It is forbidden to drive any vehicle past this notice."

I did it once before; I still remember the rising sun, (it was only 6am.) the purple, dew-laden heather, the rabbits which were scooting from under my very wheels; and the wonderful panorama stretching into the distance.

Here

Can a car be unlucky? The following brief history would seem to indicate that it can.

(O)n June 28th, 1914 a large red German car containing the Archduke Francis Ferdinand who was driving in state when a bomb was thrown at it without, however, damaging either the car or it's occupant. The Archduke, unfortunately, with his wife, was killed later the same day. During the Great War the car remained in the Vienna Museum.

(A)fter the war the car was sold. Many accidents followed, the owner finally being killed in it.

There

(T)he car then went from Bosnia to Transylvania but could not be sold because of it's evil reputation. It was therefore hired out, but few people would drive it. In 1926 the car was being driven by it's owner to his daughter's wedding. It never arrived.

(T)he final tragedy which this fated car brought about, revealed itself, — the owner and three friends being killed outright in a crash.

(T)his unlucky red car was then broken up and burnt.

(I)nformation concerning the production of

Continued on page 33.

MOTORING IN N E

What strange coincidences life brings! Since I wrote the first part of this story a month ago, I have had a letter from my sister in which she tells me that the man I mentioned who gave us the robe, Abraham Washner, has been elected Mayor of Invercargill, a prosperous little city of about 25.000 in the south of New Zealand!

The next day after our arrival at Manapouri we picnicked along the banks of the Warow River during the morning. This river connects the lakes Anav and Manapouri, and then flows from Manapouri to the sea, a distance of about 50 to 60 miles. The lake is 692 feet above sea level so the river is swift. The country drained by it has a high rainfall, and includes many large glaciers, which makes the volume of water large and keeps it steady. The banks of the river are high, sometimes over 100 feet, and when in flood it never overflows them. Between the two lakes there is a part known as Horseshoe Bend, where the river sweeps round in an almost perfect horseshoe, a favourite camping spot. There is no bank to speak of on the inner side of the shoe, but on the outer side the bank is about 100 feet high, and

W ZEALAND

PADRE Mc. DOWELL.

covered with a young brush forest. The stone over which the river flows is greenish, and the fast flowing clear water is given a dark green appearance by this together with the reflected colour of the forest on the bank. Where the water breaks over the stones there are slashes of white which remind one of the "green-stone" used in ornament, and peculiar to certain parts of the country. This stone varies from almost transparent green to very dark green, and when polished is very beautiful.

After lunch we made our way down the river over tracks which could not possibly be honoured with the name road. The tributaries of the Waiaw were not then bridged and the fords were often made almost impassable by spates which brought down large boulders and strewed them over the crossings. Sometimes the first car would get stuck and we would pull it back out again with the rope. Sometimes the second, and we would then pull it through. On one occasion the back axle caught on a boulder, rode up on to it with the impact, and we were stranded with the back wheels spinning in the air. There was nothing for it but to get into the ice cold water and lift it off.

Continued on page 34.

490 ccs Racing International Model.

This is a machine specially designed for racing and it's record in the sporting world speaks for itself.

Every engine is built and specially tuned in Norton's experimental de-partment, each engine is bench-tested and has to pull a pre-determined load before being passed out as suitable for building into the complete machine. An aluminium alloy head and barrel is fitted as standard: an electron

Continued on page 28.

SUMMARY of the
IDEAL CAR

The 1944 "Phorbee 12" has come — and is going to stay. What's more — it's sold well!

Born in violent argument, produced by hand-craftsmen in anxious hope, the "Ideal Car" was received by Stalag with an astonished silence. This unobtrusive "M.M.C." had punched the camp's motorists on the nose! Then the argument started.....!

From thinking and sensible readers the car evoked only praise and warm appreciation for the whole scheme and it's execution. The majority of British owners' opinion and Dominion drivers with wide understanding were solidly in support of the "Phorbee 12" and, on discussion, with almost it's entire specification. Universally, readers acclaimed the 'utility' points of the specification and it's practical convenience.

Criticism was mainly on the lines that; the body was far too 'extreme' in streamline; had too much overhang; would weigh too much for a '12' engine; would cost too much; was too low-powered for export (it was thereupon explained that it was mainly for domestic absorption); was too big and heavy; would use too much petrol if used 'blown'—(whereupon it was explained that the body was only pressed panelling and a blower could be used to give the old performance for less throttle.)

A garage owner: "I think it a bad feature to take your final drive off the layshaft! Your ground clearance is too little and the car too long— how many owners can afford 17 ft. garage space? Isn't that going to make it hard to park in city traffic? Your doors are too long and are going to be awkward to use in busy pavements. How do you get the back wheels off?"

A heavy haulage man: "Too big and heavy for the majority of British owners—

they prefer 8 to 9 h.p. and your British buyer will have a first rate engine; body lines don't matter. Yes— I run a Ford 8 and a motor cycle."

Specialist: "Why not a Deisel motor? Yes — deisel's my job, but I think you could make a deisel small enough and smooth enough and you should be able to mass - produce it cheaply. Deisel would give you higher performance and cheaper running. I'm sure modern metals with their higher U. T. S. are capable of lighter constructions, so cutting down the weight of the bulky castings hitherto needed in C. I. due to the high compressions. This high wt/ h.p. has so far been a big disadvantage to us."

Others said: "Brake and gear on the right is 'one too many'; "Why not use six volt— even in America they get through the winter on six volts, twelve volts is too much." "Turbo-booster would not feed properly at ground level." "Why hasn't it a self-change, automatic change only needs five governors." "You'd never make it for £250." "Why use a Riley type motor, surely it would be too costly and is unnecessary except for sports cars. I would plump for a s.v. 6-cylinder." "A blower would cost too much, shorten motor life and how about consumption?" "What about Rover type one-shot

auto-lubrication of the chassis from the clutch pedal and an accelerator-starter." "Streamline bodies are difficult to work on at the rear (?)" "Are you going to make it of plastics?"

There was a marked body of opinion, however, which said, "a very good idea, I would very much like to see a '12' produced on these lines – it would be a very fine little job. Perhaps Hillman or Morris could do it."

Quite a number of people wanted to place orders. As for those Blighty readers who said the Wolseley was "the only vehicle looking like a car on the page" – and the Trans-

Continued on page 35.

EASTERN INTERLUDE

by Tom Swallow

At 10.am sharp the Pontiac pulled up outside my hotel and I was "hauled" aboard. No amount of persuasion would win for me the seat behind the wheel, nor the one next to it. "Not on your life" I was told "You're sitting here with us" and although I can assure you the fair sex has no influence over me whatsoever, I sat in the rear --- and liked it.

It was cold, but the sun was shining as we skirted the ancient walls of the Holy City and passed the Damascus Gate where a sheep market has been held for over 2,000 years. The road descended steeply into Kedron Valley and as we passed the Gardens of Gethsemane a lower gear was engaged and the long climb to Bethany began.

Leaving Bethany behind we continued along the well metalled roads which were so steep that they often necessitated second or even bottom gear to act in a braking capacity. The sparse "mossy" vegetation became thinner and thinner with each turn of the wheel and by the time the "Good Samaritan Inn" had been passed the countryside had taken on the aspect of a real wilderness.

Except for a couple of police armoured cars (Ford V8s) and a camel caraven the road was deserted. A stop was made at the "Sea Level" sign and a photograph was taken of this tri-lingual, bullet-holed sign, which is used as a target by passing troops.

Would you like to take over?" I was asked. "Of course" I replied. "No he wouldn't," said a pair of feminine voices. "I most certainly shall" I countered firmly.

When we continued our drive I was able to observe (from my seat in the rear!) that the road was continuously diving under the lee of 'cliffs' that had been blasted into the side of the hills, which by now bore more and more signs of having been the sea-bottom many years ago.

At last we shot out into open ground and the speedo was soon telling a different story along the lowest road in the world, 1,300 feet below sea level.

We pulled up at the "Haliyah", a cafe on the edge of the Dead Sea, and made our way to the pebble beach.

I suddenly realised that it was hot and that the glassy sea looked very inviting. "Let's have a swim" said one of the girls

"1 haven't brought a costume."
"Then hire one." "Not on
your life" I hastened to
reply, having seen some of
the faded, moth-eaten
costumes that were offered
for hire. As we entered the
water I was struck by the
strength of the brine and
soon regretted having shaved
that morning. Was my neck
tingling!

After floating around
for an hour or so
we left the water and were
covered from head to foot

with a considerable layer of
salt as soon as the brine
dried on us.

The picnic lunch. →
I will spare you the
details — was followed by
tea in the Halijah during
which meal some villainous
looking banana jam was
served.

Just as it was getting
dark we climbed aboard
and were seen off by (it seemed from the noise) a million
frogs and crickets.

Back in Jerusalem it
was quite cold and
I had to admit to my captors,
one each side, that one could
have an enjoyable time as
a passenger, even in a
Yankee car·····!

AUSTIN
RACING CAR

by Maurice Airay

Since it's inception in 1922 the Austin Seven, owing to it's remarkably simple design, has met with great favour amongst sporting enthusiasts who found that it was capable of putting up a creditable performance for it's size. Various sports models have appeared, including the Gordon-England, Brooklands and Ulster types which have achieved considerable fame all over the world not only in races but also by breaking records.

A noteworthy success was scored in the 1930 500 miles race when S.C.H. Davies drove a specially tuned Brooklands model into first place. At the same time enthusiasts were constantly modifying what was essentially a sports car for participation in racing events.

It was towards the end of 1934 that the factory produced a specially streamlined model designed by T. Murray Jamieson to attack class 'H' records which had been the monopoly of the M.G. Midget. With the designer at the wheel the car successfully broke Worlds 750 c.c. records for the mile and kilometer.

Around this time there appeared from the Austin works another extremely neat single-seater which had been built specifically for actual road and hill-climb events. In due course this car was sent to Germany where in the capable hands of such exponents as Maurice Baumer (who later became a member of the Mercédés Grand Prix Team) and E. G. Burgaller it gained quite a reputation for itself. On it's return to England, the car's white colour was changed to light blue when it was used to good effect by Mrs. K. Petrie. This car had a side-valve motor.

The now famous 750c.c. Austin Racing Model

was undergoing it's final trials in November 1935 with T. Murray Jamieson, it's designer at the wheel.

In comparison with previous Austin models, the design may perhaps be regarded as revolutionary. Having a cubic capacity of 744, the engine departed from normal Austin practise in that the valves were operated by twin overhead camshafts, while the crankshaft was carried on three bearings. Sucking through a S.U. carburettor, the Murray Jamieson "blower" was mounted vertically and housed at the rear of the power unit.

An extremely narrow chassis was under-slung both fore and aft a a system of non-independent suspension being used. The tubular front axle was supported by a single transverse spring quart-elliptic springs were employed.* Large diameter brake drums were fitted to all four wheels, the brakes themselves being operated mechanically by both foot and hand.

* on the rear.

cowling and terminating in a streamlined tail incorporating a head rest and housing the fuel tank, the "monoposto" body was of compact and neat proportions. The driver was enabled to sit fairly low by reason of the worm drive rear axle; the gear lever to the 'crash' type box being situated on the left and the handbrake on the right outside the body.

Commencing in a neat rounded radiator

Pat Driscoll, Charles Dodson, and Charles Goodacre handled the new cars in their first races. The 'works' team usually consisted of two of the new cars and the older side valve model which Mrs. Kay Petrie drove. This latter car was driven effectively on one occasion by 'B. Bira' at Donnington.

Perhaps in the hands of Albert Hadley and Charles Dodson the Austin racing car has enjoyed the most measure of success. Every-where it has appeared, at Brooklands, Donnington and Crystal Palace, at Shelsley Walsh and Prescott it has proved unbeatable in it's class The engine has, on the test-bench, achieved 12,000. r.p.m.

The Austin's diminutive size should in no way detract from the greatness of it's achievement for in it's class it is comparable favourably with the Grand Prix Mercédés Benz.

Norton (CONTD).

crankcase; B.T.H. racing magneto and also a T.T. remote control carburettor.

Norton spring frame is employed; petrol tank of 4¼ gals. capacity finished in dull plate, quick-lift filler caps are used. Straight through exhaust pipe with meg-aphone, cone type front brake, Dunlop racing tyres; long levers, racing mud- and chainguards; special racing gearbox with-out kickstarter, incorporating three- plate clutch.

TEMPERING STEEL

AND IDENTIFICATION CHART

Tempering is the method of bringing a piece of carbon tool steel to the correct degree of hardness and toughness for it's particular job. The harder it is made, the more brittle it becomes.

A woodworker's chisel, for example, has to be tempered so that it is hard enough to keep it's edge when sharpened; but tough enough to withstand knots in the wood and sudden mallet blows on the handle.

It is easy to confuse the three varieties of iron and steel: wrought iron, mild steel and cast steel. Neither wrought iron nor mild steel can be tempered. It is advisable to keep cast steel apart from mild steel so that confusion cannot arise.

Having made certain that the metal to be tempered is Cast Steel, the first step is to soften it, in order that it may be worked with files and drills, etc. to the required shape. Heat the metal to redness and bury it in cinders or ashes so that it cools as slowly as possible.

It may then be worked to shape. The following table gives details of some simple tests which may be carried out to distinguish the three varieties of Iron:

Test	Wrought Iron	Mild Steel	Cast Steel
Sound when dropped on stone or concrete.	Dull note.	Medium note.	Ringing note.
Cut partly thro' metal and bend.	Bends well. Hard to break.	Bends well; but then breaks off sharply.	Bends very little. Breaks with loud snap.
Heat to redness; cool quickly in water; test with file	No change.	No change, but occasionally slightly harder.	Becomes very hard and brittle.
Clean a small area drop a spot of Nitric Acid on it.	Green stain.	Brown stain.	Dark Brown to Black stain.

"Get off the road!"

"OH AL! HAVE YOU A FEEDING CHART FOR A BABY AUSTIN."

"Its obviously copied from a *Pontifrack* Hudsons make it"

That in 1906 there was a motor race from Pekin to Paris.

The event was organised by the French newspaper "Le Matin" and five machines crossed the starting line. They were a 40 h.p. Itala, a 15 h.p. Stykes, two de Dions and a 6 h.p. "Trike". The Itala (Prince Borghere) crossed the winning line some two months later, after a very difficult period in Siberian mud, sand and mountain passes. When crossing a bridge, his car caused it to collapse, which in turn shattered a wheel, this was eventually repaired by a native blacksmith and so enabled the Prince to carry on and win.

Do you know?

That a steam bus with a seating capacity of 130 travelled from Ipswich to Edinburgh and back in 1871.

The vehicle was 60 feet long, seating 60 people inside and 70 on the top deck. The average speed for the whole journey was 6 m.p.h. On one straight stretch near Doncaster 25 m.p.h. was recorded, cruising speed was in the region of 20 m.p.h.

The only accident occurred in Dean Street, Newcastle, when the bus got out of control on the muddy hill, turned broad-side, and carried everything before it.

(T)he bus was later sent to India where it was in operation for a number of years as a passeng-er carrying vehicle.

Here & There
(CONTINUED)

new cars seems to vary slightly, one informant say-ing that new cars are not being produced for civilian purposes but a letter dated June refers to a "brand new" Hillman '10' that had just been purchased. Next month we will know who was correct.

(A) two-stroke motor cycle stood near the new well in "D" North com-pound; the usual crowd was having a debate as to 'what' it was. One knowing fellow (not a member of the MMC) stated emphatically that the fuel was diesel (there was a little residue on the carb.) while another was quite con-fident that it was petrol because he had taken a 'sniff' in the tank.

(O)f twenty N.C.O's. not one seemed to know that petrol and oil mixed, was the usual fuel for two-strokes.

NEW ZEALAND
(CONTD.)

some of the metal work was dented a bit but 'mum's the word'.

At one point we had to climb a hill with a clay surface. A convenient spring near the top fed the rather miserable grass growing on the road-way, and made the surface beauti- fully greasy. It was all hands out to push, and we just made it.

Near here we visited an electric power station built on the banks of the river. The fall of the water is only down the bank, at this place about 70 to 80 feet high. The supply comes from a small lake about four miles away, and I shall never forget the impression made on me as I stood on the river bank with the great body of water sweeping past. The workers in the power house told us that the normal speed of the current at this place was 15 m.p.h; it was really awe inspiring. Attempts were made to bring material for this power house upstream from the river mouth twenty miles away, but no launches could make headway against the stream.

A fine tea at Quatapira and a merry drive home in the late evening, tired and hungry, to enjoy such a meal as I am looking forward to one of these days again soon.

Hints & Tips

Tappet adjustment.

An easy method of adjusting tappets on a 4-cyl. engine is as follows:—

Open fully no.8 valve & adjust no.1 valve.

" " no.7 " " " no.2 "

In all cases the sum of the numbers of both valves adds to 9. In the case of a 6-cyl. engine employing 12 valves, 13 is the number to be arrived at.

To determine polarity. Should a battery be unmarked and the positive and negative terminals unconnected, a certain method of determining + from − is as follows:—

Emmerse both battery wires into a solution of salt and water, when the − lead will be observed to 'gas' freely. This also applies to an unmarked dynamo; proceedure in which case is to start up, drop the dynamo leads into the solution. The same chemical reaction will take place.

Continued from page 21. —atlantites who wondered "what that comic green thing in the middle was", and the earnest folk who wanted to know "why they were all 3-wheelers?" (Oh! Tommy Rodger —!) We'll leave them with the 'expert' who identified (with emphasis) one body as "the Pontefrack — you know, made by Hudson about '37." . . . .

CLUB

The final round of the Quiz resulted in a win for the Rudge team making the final results as under.
Rudge 98¾, Morgan 83, Ford 78¾, Alvis 65½, Plymouth 59½, Tanks 59.

I think all will agree that the quiz series proved to be of a very interesting and instructive nature. Not many of us knew that a Morgan 3-whlr. fitted with reversing gear, is classed as a car. But we know now.

The winners of the competition are to be congratulated on a good performance, as are all who took part.

A recent letter from England brings the information that C.S.M. Domulo's "Special," the one he built himself, was in service until twelve months ago. It is now on jacks at his home and 'yours truly' has been promised a 'jangle'. Roll on the day. Jack is putting his 'art' to the test here in IV.b. and is producing a replica of the 'Matilda' tank. The engine comes from a gramophone, it is to be hoped that he will finish it in time for us to report on a 'road test'.

"Motor cycle 'Trials and Trials Riding" by A.C. Bourne is now available to club members. If you wish to read this very useful publication give your name to Allan Vidow our

NEWS

"circulation manager."

●**M**aurice Airey and Bill Trevett who are the latest additions to the committee need no introduction

●**M**aurice gave us the excellent talk on Motor Racing some time ago and took a great part in the discussions on our 'brain child' the Ideal Car and is well known to us all.

●**B**ill was responsible for half of the drawings of the 'Phorbee Special' and it is to be hoped that we shall soon be able 'to get the bit into his mouth' and make him talk.

●**T**he Rudge Radial head has been redesigned several times by two of our members, to reduce mechanical noise. One design by a very famous member, could be described as being fitted with four o.h. camshafts driven by a common shaft and a terrific wheel which covers the whole head. The plug "lives in a little hole" in the centre and the machine is guaranteed to be 100% improvement on the exhaust note of the D.K.W. Yes! he's been a prisoner three years now. "'Nuff said."

●

All Club enquiries to:-
T. Swallow,   Hut 53.b.
A. Pill,   Hut 47.a.

38.

Famous Last Words
"As a matter of fact, I drive better when I've had a couple."

Here's one who always deprecates
Snug cars; unnecessary weights,
His voice decries when he is roused,
Those who travel thus "glasshoused",
But he, 'skin clad from head to heel,
Enjoys with everlasting zeal
All weathers fair and foul alike,
Mounted upon his motor-bike.
From what he says you'll easily judge,
Tom Swallow always rides a Rudge.

P.J.Benrose

Famous Last Words

"Ar Last, darling."

USED MACHINE MART.

B.S.A. Aug 1939. 249 c.c. o.h.v. de Luxe. Foot change etc.. 49 gns.	Rudge Sports Special 500 c.c. 1938 very fast 58 gns.
B.S.A. 1940 side valve model C.10. 250 c.c. 43 gns.	Ariel Red Hunter 2-port 250 c.c. 1937 45 gns.
B.S.A. 1937 s.v. de Luxe 600 c.c. Saloon s/c. 58 gns.	Norton Model 16H 500 c.c. 1936 49 gns.
Coventry Eagle. Dec. 1940 148 c.c. 6,000 miles only 35 gns.	New Imperial 500 c.c. Very little used 1939 52 gns.
Coventry Eagle 1935 o.h.v. J.A.P. 2 port 250 c.c. 26 gns.	A.J.S. 2-port o.h.v. 350 c.c. new tyres. 1936 42 gns.
Douglas 596 c.c. comb. Swallow 2/str. saloon; 1939. 79 gns	Sunbeam de Luxe 350 c.c. o.h.v. 1934. good finish. 28 gns.
P&M. 598 c.c. Redwing '100' 2/str. comb. small mileage. 85 gns	O.K. Supreme o.h.v. J.A.P 250 c.c. 1936. 26 gns.
Rudge Rapid 245 c.c. o.h.v. 939 good cond. 52 gns.	All machines overhauled and guaranteed.

All above prices can be taken as a true indication of the used machine market up to May 1944.
Prices ex. "The Motor Cycle."

THE SUPER SPIRIT

~ Contents ~

49

The FLYWHEEL

NUMBER SIX

"KEEPS THE WORKS GOING ROUND ON THE IDLE STROKES"

STALAG 4B · OCTOBER 1944 · GERMANY

Strictly speaking, we should have followed up our Show Number with a "Buyer's Guide" and / or a "New Motorist's Number." That is the usual procedure in the Best Circles. Well — the Buyer's Guide came out in the Supplement, and (between ourselves) the production of a New Motorist's Number would call for rather more imaginative detail mechanical drawings than we're capable of. Instead, we've

"went all streamlined" and gone so fast even Vidow nearly caught himself up with the Supplement!

It's good to see membership keeping up in a most gratifying way. So often enthusiasts talk themselves right out "in the wire"... and then interest flags, numbers drop, and the survivors feel horribly depressed and hopeless.

On this topic it seems the place now to note with

satisfaction how the super-energetic efforts of "our Herculean Tommy" and the patient, unseen stage managing of the industrious and un-discourageable "Arfer" have brought deserved fruit: — Good but tongue-tied members have been brought out of themselves: developed into able and generously informative speakers — for everybody's good.

We exist to amuse ourselves and to learn. It's been good fun, these last nine months.

What all this leads to is that it's up to the new members not to sit back and just "absorb" — they've got to get on their feet, too, and keep the fire going. You don't know what you can do until you try — and some of the older members have surprised themselves (and us!) And they've come back for more.

We not only expect you, each one, to find some angle of your black and dubious past to amuse us with, but to keep your ears flapping for any rider or driver who might be stimulated into a keen and entertaining member (and possible talker) by a little quiet, peppy prodding. So very many fellows have no idea they can be interesting to others: keep listening and drag 'em along. (If you doubt your ability to wriggle their secrets out of them, some of the old committee members are expert "wormer-outers."....).

Editor

It is considered by our World's Land Speed record holders that it is not safe to attempt a world's record on normal road surfaces; they like a road with at least ¼ of a mile in width, in which to manoeuvre their cars in the event of any unforeseen occurrence.

I imagine that one of the strongest upholders of this opinion is Sir Malcolm Campbell, who, undoubtedly owes his life to the fact that he had plenty of room when breaking the world's record at Daytona in 1928. He writes..... "On my first run I entered the measured mile at a speed of 210 m.p.h., and just as we were leaving the end of the course I looked down at my instruments and saw that they were registering 220 m.p.h.....

Suddenly, without any warning, we hit a hummock on the course, the car leapt into the air, and I was almost thrown out, as in those days I was not strapped into my seat. I received the full blast of wind in my face, my goggles were blown off, and next moment the car was broadsiding into the soft sand — all this taking place in full view of the spectators. I was certain that the end had come, for the car was almost out of control and was heading for the dunes, ploughing its way throu soft sand. Instead of wrenching the wheel hard over I gradually worked the car on to the hard surface once more, but I had travelled a mile before I succeeded in getting her back on the course again."

.... Phew, some broadside!.

Speaking of records, it is not generally known that we have a record holder in the ranks of the Mühlberg Motor Club. It's a fact. Pat H.J. holds the "altitude record" (M.T.) in South Africa. Mounted on an Excelsior 172 c.c. Villiers "Brooklands"-engined motor cycle, he climbed up Monte-aux-Sources (11,700 feet high, the highest peak in S.A.) to a height of 8,500 feet. At this altitude he was forced to abandon his attempt, owing to hunger and the boulder-strewn nature of the surface and — but that's another story, we'll get him to write it out for a later issue.

Received by recent mail..... A Standard "9", new in 1938 priced £160 — was purchased last month for .....£270. Of course, it is only six years old. Yes! I think that more than a few car enthusiasts will re-enlist in the two-wheeled ranks. You see, motor cycles are only approx. 8% above their '39 cost.

The History of the MG

by P. C. HARRINGTON-JOHNSON

The letters "M.G." stand for "Morris Garages" — a servicing department of the plant managed (in the middle '20s) by Mr. Cecil Kimber. A Morris enthusiast himself, he knocked together a "different" Morris, using a "bull-nose" chassis of the 11·9 h.p. four cylinder, 3 speed, stock car, and with "gutter" mudguards of tinplate, longer scuttle, less dumpy tail and wire wheels — produced quite a fast-looking and attractive model with a slightly better performance than any other Morris Cowley car of this date.

The car was quickly spotted by a keen Morris owner and Kimber sold it at a profit. Why shouldn't he do this as a regular thing? The result — soon after Morris had taken over the Wolseley plant with its higher performance engines — was the M.G. Car Co., around 1927, to market a car of sporting type on the parent Morris chassis.

Most famous of these

early cars were the "18/80" six – looking not unlike a sports "Dominion" Morris — and the immortal "D" Midget – a two-seater boat-tail with the 850 c.c. camshaft four-cylinder motor developed out of the famous 10/23 Wolseley (who probably took the design from the Wolseley "Viper"– Hispano-Suiza 200 h.p. V8 aero engine of last war "fighter" days.)

(and the bigger had sweeping scanty guards) the baby – a fabric body, cycle-type wings and a louvred valance along the side of the chassis. Spring-spoke steering and finned brake drums were used. Instead of Rudge wheels, the normal 3-bolt Morris type were fitted and normal 3-speed gearbox to the Midget, though a year or two later the "M" Midget appeared with

Typical of sports-car style of those days, the cars had twin carburettors, V-screens, stayed headlamps

a 4-speed remote-change. With the "M", the Mark II Six came out. These machines would do 65-75 m.p.h (8 h.p)

B.T.

a 1,087 c.c. camshaft six, which came out in the M.G. as the "F" Magna — an "overgrown" "D" type with similar "trimmings" on a longer chassis. It was followed almost at once by the "L" Magna — in which the inlet ports were on the driver's and the exhausts on the other side of the head (an essential if an engine is to go really rapidly).

and 85 (six).

They were sterling cars. The Midget proved an excellent competition car and some 750 c.c. models were made for a factory team to battle with the Austins. They sold all over the world and from New Zealand to Scotland some are still running (with 150-200,000 miles "on the clock"!) Brooklands and Road circuits in Ireland brought early 'scalps' to the firm.

About 1930 Wolseley produced the Hornet,

About 1931-2 the immortal Magnette came out — (first, the K1, then the K2 and K3) a tuned "L" Magna. It leaped to success with Nuvolari, Lord Howe and the unlucky Norman Black in the T.T.

(the first small car "il maestro" had ever driven, and he liked it!) Dick Seaman, Whitney Straight and Bira began their racing careers on these fast and sturdy, longish little cars.

M.G. began to mean something. The letters stood out against a growing and glowing blaze of glory. Racing successes too numerous to recount followed in a continual stream from every part of the world. Whoever wished victory in 1,100 c.c. racing drove M.G. – if he wanted a sporting chance. The firm was building a reputation probably unique in history.

Early in the '30's the style changed. The Midget changed its cylinder head to the faster type, underslung the chassis at the rear and adopted the "International Formula" racing four-seater body with two seats and a flat box tail and tank. This came out as the "J," with upswept scuttle, windflares, cycle-type guards, flat folding screen and five Rudge wheels. The speed was 75 - 80 m.p.h. The range was then the Midget (850 c.c.),

B.T.

Magnette (1,087 c.c.) and the 2 litre six (Mark II) — the last a sporting open-or-closed body model. The other two could be — and were — raced "off the floor."

Racing produced the "J4," with a Roots blower mounted between the dumbirons in front of the radiator — capable of 104 m.p.h. from a two-bearing crankshaft — no mean achievement. A series of "Magic Midgets" snapped up world's class records all over Europe in a continuous stream. The blaze of glory grew.

About 1934 a new series came out showing more refined taste in sports motors, and the Midget came out as the "P", with a three-bearing crank. The Magnette "grew up" to 1,287 c.c., as the "N" type. Both cars had flowing, graceful wings, far more elaborate and de luxe specification, oil filters, four seater bodies and hydraulic in place of Hartford dampers. Bodywork was coachbuilt and graceful, rev-counters were fitted in place of speedometers, and really comfortable hoods and screens were featured. More elegance and less the stark necessities was the keynote, and the famous octagon motif was lavishly used. everywhere it could be employed; even pistons would have been octagonal if it could have been done! All models did 85-90 m.p.h.

The cars (850 and 1287), however,

remained true racers at bottom and brought excellent results — the keynote of M.G.'s success perhaps — with no more than stripping, raising compression and tuning. The remarkable claim was borne out up to the eve of this war by an unequalled list of amateur-driver racing successes, even with second-hand cars.

The "P" was broadened into the "PA" and "PB" cars, 850 and 950 c.c. and a special racing "Q" type was made, — which appeared 'blown', with successes on road and track. Finally, the special

"Baby Grand Prix" "R" type arrived, a single seater, pre-selector gear, torsion sprung (independant-all-round) with a high-pressure blower and a 750 bronze-head motor capable of around 120 m.p.h. Never properly completed — it was still giving teething troubles when Lord Nuffield bought Kimber out, about 1937 — only a few were built but these have done well for owners devoting the time (1-2 years!!) to get the best from their tricky and sensitive organisms.

New management spelled" the death of M.G. as a car to be reckoned with in truly sporting circles. Racing was dropped and the range was "clarified" to the "T" Midget, 1300 c.c. 4 cyl. pushrod two seater, 1½ litre 4 cyl. pushrod four seater, a 2 litre (S type) and in 1938 – 2½ litre pushrod 6 cyl. smart, sporty looking cars, with handsome open and closed coach bodywork. All give 85 – 90 m.p.h. but it is not advisable to race any of the range. The motive idea behind the cars has completely changed.

Before closing, mention must be made of the fantastic "Magic Magnette": that ultra-streamlined and wonder tuned 1,087 c.c. six which on Frankfort Autobahn took world's 1,100 cc. class records at 197 m.p.h., was rebored "over the week-end" at the roadside, and badly shook German Grand Prix technicians – proud of 260 m.p.h with 3-4 litre Mercedes G/P. cars – by clocking 212 m. p.h. from 1,104 (or so) c.c. as a "1500"-class job. A sister 750 c.c. six is in vaseline now for a 180 m. p.h. try...!

Artist's impressions by

Dudley Mumford
Bill Trevvett

Henne does it!

After a cold night the morning of Nov. 28 1937, revealed a group of officials tensely watching the preparation of a two-wheeled vehicle. Three men started pushing, a crescendo of exhaust roar was heard and the fish-shaped machine flashed away.

On the Munich Autobahn

The scene on the Munich Autobahn later became clearer when it was announced to the world that Ernst Henne, riding a 500 c.c. B.M.W. (supercharged horizontally-opposed twin-cylinder, shaft driven, sprung-frame and partially streamlined), had broken the world's record for motor cycles at 276·282. klms. per hour. On the same morning he proceeded to clean up twelve other class records, all with a comfortable margin.

This record-breaking business calls for a great amount of research; a glimpse of some of the difficulties to be surmounted would be of interest.

The three greatest exponents of motorcycle maximum speeds of those days were Tarrufi (Italy) Fernihough (England) and Henne (Germany). All three were of the opinion that 165-170 m.p.h was the difficult period to overcome in seeking maximum honours. The difficulty was not so much the h.p which an engine could develop as the stabalising of the machine at those speeds.

Coincidental with the breaking of the maximum record, a German stream-line theorist, Zencominierski, published an article in a motoring paper maintaining that a streamlined body must have as little frontal resistance as possible,

pointing out that suction caused by the tail was adding to the disadvantage already set up by using a streamlined body. He theorised in two ways, an unstreamlined bike had little frontal pressure to overcome, but the rider was exposed. The streamlined machine had a greater resistance area in the front to overcome and also rear airflow suction— caused through this. He summarised by saying that a longer and larger tail should be used.

The B.M.W. broke the record without a "lid" -better balance, and rider's visibility was obtained without it. Two verticle stabalising fins, which, when spread out and combined with a longer tail, helped still more to hold the machine down.

FASTEST ON EARTH

by M. T. Airey

When, one day in 1939, Captain G. E. T. Eyston driving his "Thunderbolt" car set up a new World's Land Speed Record of 373 m.p.h.—he demon-

U.S.A. where under favourable conditions a clear straight run of 13 miles may be obtained. For records of this type a flying start is employed and

strated convincingly Britain's superiority in this field. The present record was established at the Bonneville Salt Flats, Utah,

the final figure arrived at is the aggregate of two runs, one in each direction so that no advantage may be gained from wind and gradient – although there are special regulations governing the latter.

By normal standards, Eyston's car "Thunderbolt" is certainly something of an oversize. Weighing over seven tons, it has two engines whose combined capacity totals 73 litres! Naturally to develope a smaller engine for the attempt would involve several years of careful research as well as a considerable amount of money. In consequence, the designer uses the most powerful engines obtainable which may conveniently be housed within a chassis having certain limited requirements of track and wheelbase. The two huge Rolls Royce aero engines chosen for "Thunderbolt" are placed side by side in the centre of a girder - section chassis which is carried on eight wheels.

The value of Eyston's achievement is often underestimated by some people who maintain that such a record is not, in fact, of any benefit for the motor industry. This, of course, is quite incorrect.

Much research has been carried out and much valuable information gained by the Dunlop firm to produce a tyre which will withstand the great stresses imposed by speeds around six miles per minute – when the 700 × 31 tyre, as used by Eyston, will be revolving in the region of 45 times per second.

Suspension, too, received special attention. All wheels were independently sprung, the system employed being made the more effective by substantial reduction of unsprung weight, achieved by not mounting the brakes on the wheels at all.

Here again the brakes themselves were of special design. Made by Borg & Beck, they take the form of plate clutches which are liquid cooled and, at the rear, incorporated in the transmission.

The problem of designing the massive transmission unit — which has the job of transferring the prodigious power output to the rear wheels is similar to that faced by designers of certain commercial vehicles in many respects.

Not the least of these considerations is the national prestige gained, which advertises unquestionably the merits of the English motor industry and its engineers.

Streamlining, of course, becomes an increasingly important factor as speeds increase. In the "Thunderbolt" it approaches the ideal aerodynamic form having the front end blunter than the tail which is tapered and has a stabalising fin. The only protrusions of note are the two air intakes for the super-chargers, and the driver's cockpit-which is situated in front of the two engines and just aft of the twin sets of the front wheels, all of which are steered. (CONTINUED P.21)

A Gallant Attempt

by TOM SWALLOW

The world's motor cycle speed record was — until about 1936 — more or less the property of Great Britain, but the record was broken then, and is still held, by the German ace rider, Ernst Henne, mounted on a 500 c.c. supercharged and fully streamlined "twin" B.M.W., the speed attained being some 179.4 m.p.h.

Eric Fernihough of England held the record prior to this at about 169 m.p.h. and he at once set about re-building his machine to regain the record, but, unfortunately, he was a "lone-wolf" — without the backing and equipment of a large firm — and so had to curtail his development accordingly.

The engine to be used in his Brough Superior was, basically, the same as before and a very interesting unit it appears to have been. The bottom half, if my memory is not failing, was bought second-hand and was the property of the late Baragawanath, a Brooklands personality, and mounted on to this were two "500" "Dirt J.A.P." barrels and heads giving a capacity of approximately 1,000 c.c.; a supercharger was fitted and roughly 90 h.p. obtained.

Wind tunnels are very costly things to build and Eric unsuccessfully tackled the Air Ministry with a view to using one of theirs. The body therefore had to be decided upon by "trial and error," not a very pleasant thought since at such high speeds air resistance was powerful enough to bend normal handlebars.

Eric, on his original record breaking Brough Superior.

The finished model was taken down to Brooklands and after several "try-outs" a much modified body was decided upon; the streamlining of the front wheel being almost completely abandoned.

Although not entirely satisfactory, the machine was passed "O.K.", after raising the Brooklands lap record, and the model was put on a utility wagon and driven across Europe to Gyon, in Hungary, by Fernihough and his mechanic. Several such trips had to be made before the weather was even roughly favourable. Finally however, the machine was tested under uncertain conditions, (as a result the body was further modified) and given a trial run, making the final test.

Now, it must be very expensive to have an "army" of officials standing by - so an attempt was made to break the record. To comply with the rules of the F.I.C.M. it was necessary to make a double run - once up and once down the course - and the machine and rider dealt the record a nasty crack by registering approx. 185 m.p.h., the fastest ever recorded on two wheels. But tragedy rode as passenger on the return trip. The machine was struck, it is thought, by a sudden side gust of wind, the rider being lifted bodily and flung across the road, over a wall, in amongst some trees. His speed at the time is estimated to have been 180 - 190 m.p.h.

It was found, in the hospital that Eric was suffering from a fractured skull, caused by his head striking the wall; he succumbed to his injury later that day.

The machine, which continued on its way for several hundred yards, was a "write-off," and together with the dead rider's body was placed in the van and driven back to England by the mechanic. What the feelings of this man must have been can best be imagined. And so passed on a gallant rider - in the ceaseless quest for speed honours.

The record remains with Germany until we can find someone with the necessary enthusiasm, talent and money to build the record breaker. That we have several designs capable of such speeds is an acknowledged fact. There is the 500 c.c. Triumph Twin, which in supercharged form has lapped Brooklands at some 118 m.p.h. in the hands of, I think, E. Lyons. The Vincent H.R.D. "Rapide" (1,000 c.c.) in touring trim will do nearly 120 mph and the A.J.S. V-four 500 c.c. was the first machine ever to lap any road circuit at more than 100 m.p.h. (Ulster Grand Prix 1938, Walter Rusk in the saddle).

"Yes, I think — we have the man and the machine, so — here's hoping someone will have a go."

FASTEST ON EARTH

At the same time, when the record was made, it was found necessary to streamline the car further by fitting a beautifully rounded nose over the main radiator and accordingly revising the cooling system which, it is believed, used iced water.

Can it be that with further modification "Thunderbolt" will reach to 400 m.p.h.?

Flywheel Staff

EDITOR: P.C. HARRINGTON-JOHNSON ● PRODUCER: A.H. PILL ● ART: W. STOBBS
SCRIPT: T. RODGER ● CIRCULATION: A. VIDOW
PUBLISHED IN 488

THE M.M.C. RALLY "1945"

by J. Dumalo

Some 70 competitors took part in the first M.M.C. Rally from *Preston* to *Sutton*. It was a day and *Knight* affair which had been organised at considerable ex-*Spence*.

The starters, *Ainsley* and *Burgin*, had a difficult task. The competitors were basking in the smiles of many *Maidens*, and suffering the jeers of the city *Hicks*, at the same time. Finally however, order was restored and the rally began.

The teams roared off up the *Hill* with a great *Blair* of exhausts. *Vidow* soon took the lead on his supercharged *Scott*, followed closely by *Willcock* who was riding a really *Racey* looking foreign machine – as the club became strung out some skillful riding was observed.

The first spill occurred when *Callagher* and *Gibson* collided in a narrow part of *Conroy Street*. The riders were slightly injured; first aid was administered by the local copper P.C. *Harrington-Johnson*.

While passing *Holloway* Prison *Sloter* discovered that his chain was running *Loosely*. Later it became so *Slack*, that he was forced to retire. *Elliot* gave him an *Airey* wave of the hand as he roared past on his *Hurley-Davidson*. At the water splash *Mortimer* and *Simpson* came a "purler" and were forced to *Wade* out. These unfortunate chappies were given the *Bird* by some rude spectators.

Half way through it was anybodys race. The *Harvey* Brothers were putting up a grand show, but the betting appeared to be on *Matthews Orr Ketchley*. *Gutteridge* had taken the lead from *Liggett*; this was a bitter *Pill* for team leader *Rodger* to *Swallow*. Many exciting duels took place before the finish. *Trevrett* and *Clowry* were fighting for second place when they both skidded and crashed into the local *Taylor*'s shop. They were provided with stimulants from the *Fowler* Arms. *Casey* and *Hancock* were scrapping with *Watson* and *Conklin* when all four kissed wheels and ended on the *Brown* earth in a terrific heap.

Wickens and *Hawksley* roared along the finishing straight — to cross the line together. *Williams* and *Edwards* soon followed amid cheers. *Lees, Sykes* and *Taffy Davies* arrived in a bunch; each was cheered as he crossed the line and received the flag. (CONTINUED P34)

STEEL

HARDENING & TEMPERING PROCESSES

Continued

Hardening. Objects to be tempered must first be hardened. This is done by heating the metal to redness and immersing quickly in water. The metal is then as hard as it can be made.

Tempering. The metal is brightened on a piece of sandstone or emery cloth and reheated very gradually. As the metal becomes hot, colours form on the brightened surfaces and these colours give an indication of the temperature and hardness of the metal. When the right colour for the job is reached the metal is quickly plunged into water.

The chart given shows the colour at which certain tools should be quenched so that they are tempered to the correct degree of hardness and toughness.

Process of Tempering. Simple tools to be tempered have usually to be hard at the cutting edge and comparatively soft throughout the rest of their body so that they do not easily break.

There are two simple methods of obtaining this result:—

(1). The tool, say a cold

chisel for stone work, after being softened and filed to shape, is heated in a gas ring or fire to red heat for about 2" from the end. The end is then dipped in water for about 1" and rubbed quickly on a piece of sandstone to brighten it. The heat remain—ing in the body of the tool will then pass slowly towards the end, and as the colours appear the tool is quenched when the correct colour reaches the end. Thus, both hardening and tempering are accomplished at the same temperature.

Tempering Chart.

Colour.	Use.
Very light yellow.	Files, scrapers and engraving tools.
Light yellow.	Lathe tools, dies.
Yellow.	Boring tools, repoussé tools.
Brown.	Cold chisels, shears, scribers.
Dark brown.	Centre punches, stone cutting tools.
Brownish purple.	Axes, metal drills and knives.
Light purple.	Cold chisels.
Dark purple.	Screwdrivers.
Blue.	Springs, saws for wood.

"Yes! President Swallow rides a Rudge!"
(WITH APOLOGIES TO H.M.V., — RUDGE-WHITWORTH CYCLE CO.)

"High Speech"

Fourteen years a correspondent,
He writes on cars, and knows what's meant.
By all the scientific diction,
Relative to chassis friction.

In his land of bare Karoo,
The cars are big and fast and new,
Though which to buy he can't agree,
On Frazer Nash or H. R. D.

His lectures move at high-speed rate,
He never spares to illustrate,
Happily sucking at a briar,
With two spare tins to stoke the fire

Poet and writer too, and that
Summarises your old friend "Pat"
Which is now the familiar name for
P. C. Harrington-Johnson, Editor.

P. G. Bemrose —

CLUB

Many things have happened during the past few weeks to upset the smooth running of the M.M.C..

First of all, we lost our old home the "Recce" Hut, which has had to answer an urgent call. Secondly, the weather has broken up, making open air meetings impracticable, and lastly the recent influx of prisoners has made it impossible to use an empty barrack room.

But in spite of all this we continue to operate at full pressure. Our first talk of the month was by "Buzz" Lyons — about the "V12" Lagonda, and a very fine picture of automobile engineering he portrayed.

"Andy" Anderson from "Aussi" was next with a history of the Dirt Track, he being "in" on the ground floor of the "dirty game." The sport originated in his home town of West Maitland.

On Friday last we heard all about the National Rally, in the wash house of 53.b. The talk went down all right but the speaker received a terrific "bolo" when he returned to the barrack room — the "copperman" had just made the announcement "Quiet, please, the brew will be late as Tommy Swallow is giving a lecture in the wash—

N E W S.

house.... Boos, hisses and cries of "Throw him out" "Give him to the Russians" etc.. But in spite of all this the club met in the wash-house (after ousting the band) of 47a where Len Lock gave a talk on "Testing for Vincent H.R.D." As there was a lecture in 47 barrack room the door was barred, so members had to swarm through the window.

The discussion group managed to meet "aloft" in 47a, as usual (Arthur Pill's 'muckers' having been warned that their beds would not be available)

A number of "Road Tests Recalled" have been received from Graham Walker, editor of "Motor Cycling", these have been bound in folder form and put in circulation.

I am sure you will all join me in offering a very warm vote of thanks to our benefactor for the trouble he has gone to on our behalf. It is a great pity that the first batch of road tests have not arrived, but as they were not posted until July there is still hope of delivery.

DO YOU KNOW?

That "Mercury", Tom and the Quiz teams are frequently talking about—! It was a dream design for an ideal bike brought out by a young English enthusiast about 1937 or '38. He and four pals put up a little cash and made one— the idea being to see if his design worked. If they liked the result, three or four more models would be made, one for each of them.

In rough form, the bike had an "I"- section dural frame, a Scott "Flying Squirrel" motor and radiator entirely enclosed in the frame members and pro- tected from damage.

The experimental model was, by acc- ident, seen by either "The Motor Cycle" or "Motor Cycling" and was road-tested. The result was so amazing that it was decided to see if the machine could be put on the market, and it would have been one of the sensations of the '39 Show. Top speed was 90 – 100 m.p.h., acceleration was exceptionally good, comfort and handling far beyond what would be expected of an amateur's "home-brew" job. Perhaps in the near future a "Phorbee Hotchpotch" may shake home enthusiasts.

HINTS & TIPS

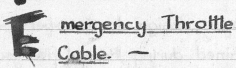

Emergency Throttle Cable. —

Should you at any time have the misfortune to break a throttle cable whilst on the road, a good substitute can be improvised easily and rapidly.

The cable usually breaks at the twist grip end; when it does, disconnect the air cable from the air slide, also the broken cable from the throttle slide, remove the air slide, fix the air cable on to the throttle slide and away you go again. —using the air lever as a throttle. Note — don't forget to replace throttle wire later.

Correct alignment of Tyres. —

When fitting a new tyre it isessential that the tyre runs true, ie., that it has no 'waves' in it. To ensure that the tyre is on straight, keep an eye on the rubber bead which is always moulded on the tyre walls. If the moulded line is parallel with the wheel rim, the the tyre is on straight.

If you have any hints, tips or other suitable articles, we shall be pleased to publish them. Contact producer A.H. Pill, hut 47a.

HOME, OR WORLD MARKET

by D. Spence. & A. Vidow.

While I was reading the article about the "Tom Thumb" motor car in a recent edition of "The Camp", Doug walked in. Motoring being our religion, it was not unusual for a discussion to develop concerning this post-war "would-be motorists" car.

Assuming that the taxation of road vehicles remains unchanged, it was voted by both of us as an answer to the prayers of thousands of prospective motorists.

Initial outlay should be no more than that of a pre-war popular "eight", for with low tax - the car being of only 6 h.p.,-combined with improved engine design due to experience gained during the last five years, "Tom Thumb" has, according to quoted figures, a petrol consumption of 60 m.p.g. with a maximum speed of 60 m.p.h.. It is the size of our pre-war "babies", and according to those who have driven the proto-type, hold a favourable comparison with them.

Motor car production ceased in 1939 This left a huge gap. The "Tom Thumb" being of small dimensions could be produced quickly for those thousands of keen users eager to spin a wheel.

It seems from the above that this car is "just the job" for the average working man's pocket.

Before airing our views to other club members we took the wise precaution of pulling our theories to pieces between us. So now, we will not only consider ourselves — but also the future of the British export trade.

Small cars are of little or no use to dominion and other overseas motorists, the American type, of large h.p. and body design, being used. Up to the outbreak of war the "British Lion" had reared its head over countries far and wide, who used cars of British manufacture.

It is common knowledge that the h.p. tax governs the size of our engines. Abolish this type of tax, and then we can use engineering science, which for years has made rapid strides but has been limited in practical use by this taxation menace.

It has been hinted that a firm in England, with a parent factory in America, have had jigs for baby cars ready for shipment from America. Does this mean that we should be content to produce cars solely for the home market?

The production of these small cars, backed by the American company in England, leaves that same company and country, no opposition for our Empire and foreign trade.

Post-war, our export trade must be developed. Therefore, in the

Motor Industry the design of our future cars, to gain any place in World markets, must be of a large engine capacity, and with suitable body lines. At the present time, the trend of design i.e. the "Tom Thumb" car — is opposite to that required for export, so destroying all possible chance of expanding this trade.

(M.M.C. RALLY)

The Mayor of *Raw-cliff* greeted the riders. He ordered the *Bell* of the town hall to be rung, and presented the winner with a silver cup in the form of a *Challis*. The Mayoress presented each rider with a *Rose*. The Mayor and Mayoress then drove away in an *Aston-Martin Carr*, through the *Woods*.

As regards *Gibb* and *Leask* and anyone of the M.M.C. who goes unmentioned in this chronicle, they were in the Rally but were probably "also rans" and maybe are still turning up the taps. A good time was had by all, and we are now waiting for the grand "Phor bee Kriegies" meeting of 1946.

SEEN IN CAMP
by Kiwi

The three cars used by the German Officers who recently visited the camp created a good deal of interest. The smallest of the three was a D.K.W., having a twin-cylinder two-stroke motor rated at 6·7 h.p.; it developes 20 b.h.p. Drive is transmitted through the front wheels and all wheels are independently sprung. The model road-tested in England before the war did 47 m.p.g., just on 60 m.p.h. and sold for £149.

The medium sized car was a Wanderer. It has a 4 cylinder O.H.V. motor rated at 13·8 h.p. and independent suspension for all four wheels, may be obtained in "blown or unblown" form, the one here being unblown. Price £580 (blown). Both makes come from the Auto Union group.

The larger of the trio, somewhat reminiscent of American design, was the Opel Admiral. Opels were built in Germany by the American General Motors Corporation. This model had a 6 cylinder O.H.V. motor of 3·6 litres capacity and about 30 h.p. (R.A.C. rating). It is the German Industry's equivalent of the American Chevrolet and British Vauxhall "25", with about the same price and comparable performance.

Essolube

Essolube MOTOR OIL

AMERICAN PETROLEUM COMPANY

MOTOR CYCLING

PROPRIETORS:

MC.GW.125.

TEMPLE PRESS LIMITED

MANAGING DIRECTOR: Roland E. Dangerfield
DIRECTOR AND GENERAL MANAGER: Robert Ashworth

DUNLOP "90"

CONTENTS

The FLYWHEEL

WINTER RIDING NUMBER

"KEEPS THE WORKS GOING ROUND ON THE IDLE STROKES"

NUMBER SEVEN • NOVEMBER 1944 • STALAG IVB • MÜHLBERG ON ELB

It seems about time we considered all this winter business. A great deal of damage to "the sport" is caused by people who, taking absolutely no precautions whatever, go through the winter months unsuitably clad for our northern climatic conditions. If their complaints of colds, flu and wet shirts remained unvoiced, then all would be well, but these hairbrains will insist on broadcasting their terrible hardships to the only-too-eager "hostile" world of motorists and pedestrians, leaving a most damaging impression that motor cycling is rough, tough or stupid.

Perhaps the better way to start a winter is to weatherproof the machine. Undoubtedly this has been done to a great extent by the manufacturer; but one can always make sure.... Some folk ride all winter — and say they like it. Others daren't. We cater for both sorts in this issue. We've even catered for those who've more sense — who, while Tommy's numbed fingers stuff spuds in his "hold" for a frosty "Exeter," are (in a sensible climate, shirt sleeves and a state of partial intoxication) settling down to watch the opening of the Grand Prix season!

Editor

NATAL SPRINT

The snarl and crackle of two machines recede as the riders disappear into the haze.

A summer breeze gently fingers their dust and passes it across the shimmering yellow veld.

A "250" snakes out of the bend and screams up the scale until, with deft change, a new gear modifies the note. Down, down, flat over the bulbous tank the rider settles himself — fumes from the filler-vent reach his dust stained nostrils.

He looks ahead between tank-top and handle-bars, the road races up towards him, races past on either side and disappears behind.

God! — the punishment the little bus is taking to-day. The front wheel spins over bump and hole, flinging loose gravel back against the fins and tarnished exhaust. The forks re-act with pneumatic drill-like movement.

He left the road in the third lap — hit an ant-hill at that — but carried on un-scathed. He is running well for a place — if only the machine will stand the racket, — steering's not right, — if only..... when CRASH!!... the road below comes up — the world seems to split on its axis. The rider through the air. The wreck of the machine, with a

CONTINUED ON P.8.

On Four Winds

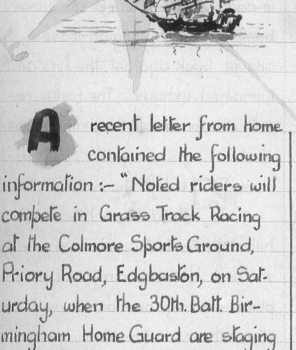

A recent letter from home contained the following information :— "Noted riders will compete in Grass Track Racing at the Colmore Sports Ground, Priory Road, Edgbaston, on Saturday, when the 30th. Batt. Birmingham Home Guard are staging a meeting on behalf of the Birmingham Accident Hospital. Among the thirty odd entrants are Oliver Bevan (B'ham), Reg Lambourne (Worcester), Ben Collins (Cheltenham), P. H. Alvis, (Coventry) and Vic Warlock (Bristol). Bert Perigo, George Rowley, Ted Mellors and G. L. Buck are among the officials."

It is nice to know that *the* sport of sports continues to flourish, it must have been grand to hear those machines go tearing around the track and to smell once more that "beautiful aroma" of dope, Castrol "R", burnt clutches and dust.

One wonders whether we shall see a 'mixed' meeting at Shelsley Walsh. There was some talk before the war of such a meeting and several well known Midland riders including O. Bevan (O.B. Special) carried out a series of tests. The bikes went up the hill in pairs and from all accounts some decent times were returned. It was thought by some that the faster bikes would be able, in a short time, to get quite near to the fastest car times.

Reading through the "Road Tests Recalled", did you notice that the Rudge "Ulster" topped the scales to some 430 lbs., whereas the Triumph "Tiger 100" scaled only 380 lbs. In spite of this the "100" was only 5 m.p.h. faster than the "Ulster" and up to 60 m.p.h. there was little difference in the acceleration.

The point is that the one machine was designed, basically, in 1930 — and the other in 1937, so that one could say that there had been very little increase in maximum speed in the intervening period. On the other hand it may suggest that there is still a lot to be obtained from the "Tiger" after a few more years development.

Talking of "Tigers", there is a smaller edition of the species which most of us have yet to see, and by all accounts will be well worth looking at. We refer, of course, to the 350 c.c. Vertical Twin.

The Frazer-Nash
by FRANK STREET

In the earlier days of motoring, Capt. A Frazer-Nash and H.R. Godfrey were jointly responsible for the introduction of the G-N, a vehicle of the cycle-car persuasion. The specification included a wooden frame, a J.A.P. V-twin motor and final drive by chains to a "solid" back axle. The motor, incidentally, was capable of turning out, unblown, 55 b.h.p. at 5,000 r.p.m. with a compression ratio of 10 to 1 and the capacity was 981 c.cs.

When, in the middle "twenties", the first Frazer-Nash cars were produced, the feature of chain transmission was retained on all models and has continued so up to the start of the war.

Of the six sports-type cars available, four have basically similar motors viz. 4 cylinder, 1½ litre. These are the Boulogne II, T.T. Replica, Ulster 100 and Shelsley, priced respectively £425, £525, £650 and £850, and capable of speeds varying from 85 m.p.h in the case of the Boulogne, to 100 m.p.h. for the Ulster, all three unsupercharged. The Shelsley, with twin Cozette blowers, has a guaranteed top speed of 105 m.p.h.

The remaining sports models are the 14 h.p.

6-cylinder Colmore, priced at £550 and the 16h.p. 6 cylinder Falcon costing £20 more. These last are not so "hot" as the 4-cyl. jobs and carry 2/3-seater bodies as compared with the strictly spartan A.I.A.C.R.-specification 2-str. bodies of the 4's. One more model completes the "Nash" range; a monoposto racing car of 4-cyl. 1½ litre capacity with twin superchargers. One of these cars, driven by A.F.P. Fane, broke the Shelsley record in '38 with a run of 38·77 seconds, a figure bettered only by a 2 litre car. £1,250 will buy such a car.

DM.

Specification of 'TT' Replica

4-cyl., 69 mm. × 100 mm., capacity 1,496 ccs.; 11·9 h.p. (R.A.C. rating); yearly tax £9 (pre-war) £15 (present); B.H.P. figure unpublished (probably 75-80 at 6,000 r.p.m.). Single o.h.camshaft (inclined valves); 3-bearing crankshaft; forced feed lubrication (wet sump); pump and fan cooling; twin S.U carbs.(30 m.p.g). mechanical and/or hand pump feed from 15½ gal. tank in tail; ignition, Bosch mag. or coil; 12 volt lighting (63 a.h.), K.L.G. plugs, unit construction of engine and single dry-plate clutch, 4 speed final drive from cross-shaft by chains (one for each ratio - dog engagement), control position optional, gear ratios to choice;

standard: top, 3·8-1; 3rd 4·7-1 2nd, 6·5-1; speed on top 95-100m.p.h; 3rd, 88 m.p.h; 2nd, 63 m.p.h; acceleration, 0-50mph. - 7⅘ secs; 0-80 - 11 secs.. Suspension, ¼ elliptics front and rear; tubular axles; mechanical brakes, 14" drums; wheelbase, 8'6" or 9'0"; track, (front) 4'0" (rear) 3'5"; length, 12'0"; ground clearance, optional - max. 10"; turning circle, 34'; weight, from 15 cwts; tyres. 18" × 5·00. Price, with T.T. type 2-str. body, £625.

◆ F N ◆

N. S.

fractured steering-lug, tears a long furrow in the road. Simultaneously the throaty roar of an overtaking "500" mingles with the uproar. A breath-taking swerve!.... the big machine clears the still moving debris, straightens out, and disappears

through the dust into nebulous infinity.

The rider lands on the back of his neck:... and "comes to" in due course. "That's one of the thrills of the Natal Sprint Circuit."

'MOGGY' PROPAGANDA

by T. Rodgers.

At our meeting on Sunday 5th Nov. we heard various club members' ideas of what a motor-cycle should be like. I was greatly impressed by the number of men who were inclined towards combinations.

Most "chair" men, perhaps owing to the fact that they have "the better half" to take around, are of the "touring" type, and, as none of us are getting any younger — better halfs included — we want more comfort than the average combination outfit provides. By the time one has bought the very popular Triumph Twin, or one of the other heavy multi-cylindered machines at a cost of about £80 solo plus an additional £20 - £25 for a good "comfortable, roomy sidecar with good locker accomodation," fitted a sidecar brake, 'stationary brake' system, handlebar muffs and all the other accessories that our combination members seem to think necessary to make the outfit ideal, a considerable amount of credits will have been swallowed up. In addition to this it is then necessary to provide oneself with an "All Weather" kit of coat, helmet, waders, gloves, goggles, etc..

My solution to the family man's problems, which I shall offer (free of charge)

is a three-wheeler. And gentle-
men, when I say three-wheeler, I
mean the one and only MORGAN.

The Morgan three-
wheeler answers all
the combination man's problems.
It gives speed, reliability, and
(most important) comfort, not only

addition to the usual driver
and passenger.

There is ample room
for luggage, and,
fitted with air cushions and a
piece of carpet on the floorboard,
one is set for a run of any
distance. The windscreen and

for the passenger but also for the
driver. There is even room for a
young child to sit on the passenger's knee, a thing which is not
advisable or practicable in a
sidecar. The "Family" model provides
accomodation for two juveniles in

hood, while not coming up to
the standard of a saloon car
give adequate protection from
wind and rain. It is also possible
to converse with one's passenger
without fitting "internal telephonic
communication" (as is almost

necessary on the modern combination with its low-slung sidecar.)

Talking with the experience of three years standing, I find the Morgan a very safe machine indeed I have travelled many thousands of miles and have never experienced any skids worthy of note, or even the slightest suggestion of overturning. I am *not* a slow driver.

The Touring model gives very little trouble, and if used at touring speeds of 40 - 50 m.p.h. gives a petrol consumption of about 50-55 m.p.g. Maximum speed is in the region of 60 m.p.h. The Super Sports model is very fast and lively. Acceleration is very good and top speed of

75-80 can be obtained from the standard job without any tuning. For really fast work the m.p.g. obtained is about 45. For the super fast driver a Roots Blower can be quickly and easily fitted at a cost of about £15 and with a bit of "hotting up" over the 100 m.p.h. mark can be reached.

The world's speed record for three-wheelers is held (I believe) by a woman on a Morgan with a speed of about 125 m.p.h.

Family man, think it over! Once you have overcome the average motor-cyclist's distrust of 3-wheelers and experienced the joys of driving and owning one, you will become as I am - A Morgan Enthusiast.

INDEPENDENT ALL ROUND
by "KIWI"

Back·before the "90's" people travelled the roads in "hay-burners" with hard springs and harder tyres; by the '20's springs and tyres were somewhat softer; a tendency carried further in the '30's; what of the '40's and '50's?

Lessons learned in racing and applied on some continental cars sold to the public before the war suggest that future production jobs will be independently sprung all round though not, probably, for some time after the war. Your mass-production car manufacturer generally fights shy of new developments till he can clearly see more coin in the coffers through adopting them. But there are good reasons for thinking that British and American makers will turn their attention to independent suspension.

It has taken a long time for manufacturers to get round to independent front suspension but even the most conservative have recognised the advantages of the system. Semi-elliptic springs and solid axles were almost universal through the '20's. Springs were stiff, shock absorbers single-acting and tyres were small-sectioned high-pressure. For sports cars even harder springs and tyres were popular and friction "shockers" were screwed up so much that "spring" in the suspension was practically stiffened out and these jobs bounced along the roads like hares taking sighting hops in new mown hay.

This trend passed its zenith when racing car makers found the current springing systems kept the back wheels off the road more than on it, leading to excessive spin with result;-loss of traction and

heavy tyre wear. Something was known of the co-relation between front and back springing and as it was easier to spring the front wheels independently than the back a start was made at the front. In a short period over the early '30's several racing cars and then more and more production vehicles came out with independent front suspension. At the same time the modern low-pressure tyre, longer and more flexible springs at the rear and readily adjustable hydraulic damper improved

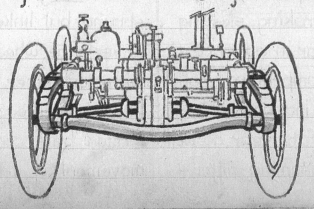

THE ORIGINAL
DE DION AXLE

road holding and riding comfort 100% over the standards of the '20's.

● Then in 1934 when the German Auto-Unions and Mercedes-Benz broke into Grand Prix racing they did so with cars which, once eased of a few teething troubles, were so much superior to rivals that they won event after event with almost monotonous regularity right up until the war. The success of the German cars was due to high power output and superb road holding — giving braking, steering and traction far in advance of any of their competitors. Both firms adopted independent suspension at the rear as well as the front, mounting differ-

entials on the chassis and driving the wheels through swinging half-shafts. In 1934 Auto-Union used swinging axles and transverse springs at the rear. Trouble at high speeds on corners was experienced with this system, due to a tendency for the back of the car to "hop" sideways. Torsion bars were substituted for the transverse springs and effected some improvement but finally the almost forgotten De Dion system was resurrected, each wheel being independently sprung but linked by a tie bar to keep the wheels in alignment with each other. The differential stayed on the chassis and torsion bars controlled the movement of the wheels.

CONTINUED ON P. 23

Laying up – or riding on?

Wet and winter riding conditions have, ever since bikes came out, been one of the biggest discouragers and most potent arguments against motor cycling. If you love the sport well (or finance compels) you will take the little extra trouble to make yourself really comfortable. It is well worth it – and the knack is easily mastered.

For the machine, three or four items of kit were available before the war which made a big difference. Legshields can be bought (price up to about £2) and – to any P.o.W. – are fairly easy to make from sheet metal. They definitely do a good deal towards keeping one's feet and legs dry. Collapsible ones were available, and a tidy idea was to fit two stubs of roller blind each side of the tank nose and pull down the shields when needed, hooking the ends to the footrests or fore engine bolts.

Several handlebar windscreens could be bought – cost up to £4 – and although looking a bit queer, certainly kept off the driving force of rain or sleet which makes one's arms and chest so cold. A windscreen also tends to relieve the rider of the burden of wind pressure and makes almost no difference at all to "sit-up" top speed It must be carefully mounted, though, or too raked an angle will cause the rider a cut nose on bumpy sections. (Americans make the very finest screens, but these are rarely seen in England)

Those numbed hands and useless fingers can be avoided completely by the use of handlebar muffs. Various types are on sale, but the bigger the better, and it is a good plan to memorise control lever positions for starting, etc., as these will be hidden in a muff. Don't let the machine's appearance

result in cold hands for you.

A feature (usually neglected) that can help, is a double or false saddle top, on the lines of the New Hudson of blessed memory. This will allow a machine to stand out in rain or snow and the rider can lift the false top and sit underneath dry and warm. An American idea that really does work is to fit a saddletop of fleece or sheepskin, and although this holds rain, it *is* warm and cosy to the "posterior."

The bike's mudguards may be valanced in with tinplate or rubberised cloth, to keep down splash, and a liberal use of grease on controls (not the handlebar end, though!) with an anti-drip device to the plug *and* advance-control wire! just about sees to that end of the job. (A good checkover of worn parts, old tyres, shaky bulbs, etc., is an insurance-policy against hold-ups in bad weather — always worse than in dry). Bald or shaky tyres and worn brakes are asking for trouble.

The main need of the rider is a sound, watertight coat. The two best are the famous Stormgard (50/-) and the Beacon "International" suit (about 55/- to 60/-). Weighing 12 lbs., the Stormgard keeps water out of the neck, cuffs, pockets and chest. Owners never wear them out — they're thrown away after about eight years as too dirty! The Beacon outfit, like the Stormgard "Sidcot" (55/-) is a water- and cold-proof boiler-suit. Worn by the British teams in the International Six Days (for which it was produced) it is well made and worth the dough.

For the head, opinions vary. A big woolly scarf or towel keeps rain from trickling down one's neck, but some prefer a beret, others a cloth cap, others a skicap, others a helmet - "higher up." Something fairly waterproof with a deep, stiff peak — to keep rain and sleet out of the eyes, is a big help. Goggles can be doped with glycerine, rubbed with potato slices (or even spittle!) to keep down misting and blobbing.

CONTINUED ON P. 20

All weather

A heavy u
of good q
slacks for the
will equip mos
quite adequate

B elstaff
Combe
suitable fo
but don't
quality

S tormgard, heavy
multi-lined coat,
incorporating tummy-pad
and patent scarf. Ideal
for all weathers. Price,
55/-. Rubber thigh
waders ensure leg pro-
tection. Average cost 15/-

S ki-cap,
leather jacket,
Bedford cord breeches
and french boots, all
combine in a smart,
cold weather outfit.

RIDING KIT

proof,
, and
r limbs
es

er
oat
weather
cheap
crack.

S idcot suit. One-piece
and fully waterproofed-
Very warm and ideal for
sidecar work etc..
Price about 65/-

B eacon
"International"
one-piece suit. Is
wind, rain and thorn proof,
ideal for all motorcycling,
especially competition work.
Price, ... 63/-

The metal-"lens" raingoggles leak through the vision slots and are draughty. Helmets with fur at neck, forehead and ears are well worth the slight extra cost.

Outside of muffs (literally) there is only one thing to be done about hands. "Procure"(?) a pair of silk gloves (ex-R.A.F. stock, 6.9ᵈ pre-war), they keep the flesh warm while oiled leather or rubber overgloves will keep them dry. Wet, soggy gloves are miserable. Mittens, grouping three or four fingers together, allow the fingers to keep each other warm.

There are any number of other and cheaper coats available. The rubber ones usually want watching for cracks and tend to make clothing worn underneath "sweat." Oilskins must be kept dressed and cool or they stick and rip. Many prefer the old cyclist's "poncho," with or without sleeves, and no front opening. A good tip is to get all such bodygear biggish. Loose fitting kit is always warmer and you can put more stuff on under it if you want to. Naturally, cheapish rubber coats can only be expected to last a couple of seasons...

For the feet and legs, probably the best are the popular waders (17/6 or so) but these look frightful and are hideously awkward if one has to walk any distance or push the bike. Snap-on leggings are a "makee-do" and generally souse your shoes sopping, but good ones can be had and they are lighter than waders and as warm. Given no cost limit, probably the best kit would be a pair of good trench boots, well polished, and slacks, worn under a Beacon "Inter" suit. Top boots, by the way can be worn under slacks or lounge trousers quite well, with long socks, and keep the feet dry even when the trousers are soaked to the knee.

Leather coats, properly dressed, are quite watertight and wonderwarm — but expensive. Electrically-heated 6 volt gloves (ex-R.A.F. stock) were a very good idea. — So is a Morgan (but you need more kit than ever — I know those Moggy hoods......!)

Finally, children, Tommy begs you won't forget the "Exeter hot potato"......

P.C. Harrington-Johnson

Club Officials

President - Tom Swallow, 53b.

Chairman-Arthur Pill, 47a,   ClubCaptain- D. Davies, 53b;

Committee:- Alan Vidow, 14b;   P.C. Harrington-Johnson, 50a;

Maurice Airey, 14b;   Bill Trevvett, 22a.

INDEPENDENT ALL ROUND

Mercedes arrived at the same system. It is by no means the last word on the subject and in the strict sense of the term it does not provide fully independent suspension for each wheel, but it was a marked advance on the conventional rigid rear axle. It enabled terrific power output to be transmitted while keeping the back wheels in contact with road surfaces having even bad irregularities, and while maintaining stability on corners.

These two concerns applied the knowledge gained through racing to ordinary production models and other German firms followed suit. In 1939 German makes with independent suspension all round were: Audi, Wanderer, Horch and D.K.W. (all Auto-Union products, Audi and D.K.W. having front wheel drive), Mercedes-Benz, B.M.W. and Adler. Various systems were used including unlinked swinging axles - which seem quite satisfactory except when used at very high speeds. It can safely be said that the road holding and riding comfort of modern German cars are superior to British and American products. Many British makers still cling lovingly to the archaic semi-elliptics and beam axles even at the front while Americans, to get smooth riding, have softened springing to the stage where stability is impaired except on modern roads specially engineered for that particular type of car.

As far as present knowledge goes, stability and soft riding can be combined efficiently only with four wheels independently

high in the first place. This will deter the stick-in-the-rut makers but their hands will be forced by the more enterprising. Independent suspension on all wheels offers many

MERCEDES REAR
WHEEL SUSPENSION

sprung so that the "jitter-bugging" of one does not affect the others. Turned out in quantities, cars independently sprung all round would cost no more than conventional ones though the cost of the change-over would be

advantages and is sounder engineering practice. It must come generally in time in the same way that racing research has given the spring forks and frame to the motor-cyclist.

STEEL Conclusion

TEMPERING & CASE HARDENING

This method is more suitable for smaller articles. The tool, say a screwdriver blade, after being softened and filed to shape is heated for about two inches from the end to red heat and then quenched. Next it is brightened and held with pliers or rested on a piece of wire. Heat is applied about one inch from the end by means of a bunsen burner. When the correct colour reaches the end the blade is quenched.

Certain tools and appliances may require to be tempered uniformly over their whole length: springs for example. This is accomplished by heating the whole object to redness, quenching completely and then brightening.

The work may then be placed on a metal plate supported over a gas ring or fire, so that the heat is applied uniformly: the colours will then form over the whole surface and the job may be quenched when the required colour appears.

A second method is to heat a piece of pipe or tube to a bright red colour and put the work inside the pipe or tube. It may be withdrawn from time to time to see if the correct colour has been reached, before quenching.

Case Hardening.

Wrought Iron and Mild Steel may be case hardened. This means that the surface is hardened to a very small depth while the core remains soft and ductile. The hardness is unlikely to go more than 1/100th of an inch below the surface, but this is sufficiently deep to withstand heavy wear and at the same time to remain tough.

The part to be hardened must be filed and finished to the required shape and size. It is then heated to redness and rolled in Potassium Ferricyanide and quenched in clean cold water. The whole operation may be repeated two or three times. A shallow metal tray is suitable for the Potassium Ferricyanide. Remember that this chemical is poisonous.

Our Library Section now contains:-

"Motor Racing."   "Road Tests Recalled."
"The Motor Vehicle."   "Motor Cycling's Handbook."
"The Autocar Handbook." "Trials & Trials Riding."
"The Road Holder." (Norton Magazine and Catalogue)
"You have been Warned."   "The Flywheel."
For details, see Club News.

"The Chair"

With orders curt he might alarm,
Then with a smile establish calm,
As he directs with endless zeal,
Smooth production of the "Flywheel."

He rode in scrambles and in trials,
His old "Red Hunter" sped the miles,
But if you want to see him win,
Boy! Wait till he gets that Triumph "Twin."

Then you'll see him fix a sidecar,
'Cause married men can never ride far
Without their spouse, which he'll require,
As soon as he's out of "the wire."

Club Howler Nº 1
"···· fitted with
Pilgrim pump deadly
loss lubrication!"

Twice a week he holds a meeting,
Using neighbours' beds for seating.
Despite all that remaining still,
Popular Chairman – Arthur Pill.

P. J. Bemrose

·CLUB

It would appear that one or two prominent members have taken to "line-shooting" around the huts. One member is trying to "spread the word" but the other, we fear, begins with words to the effect of "I was there."

That "line-shooting" has its good points is proved by the fact that an offer was received, after a line-shoot, from Joe Davies, who gave us a talk on the I.o.M. a few months ago. The offer, briefly is this. Dennis Parkinson and Joe are bosom pals and they have, in their 'stable', a bevy of 'super-super' models. Now all these are actual 'works' machines and, to cut a long story short, members of the M.M.C. who prove that they can ride such a machine are invited to receive a "kick in the pants" from a works O.K.Supreme, "G.T.S.", 350 "cammie" A.J.S.," a 250 Excelsior "Manxman or whatever may be hidden away.

During a recent talk on the "Motor Trade" did you notice a certain "war-bird" with a red neck when the rackets of car collecting was mentioned? tch.tch.

Have you a generous spirit or a "buckshee"

NEWS.

silver cup? The M.M.C. is without trophies of any kind. It would be "just the job" if we could offer a cup in, say the Scottish Six Days for the best individual performance by an ex-P.o.W. or member of the M.M.C. What do you think? Have you any ideas? If so, let's have 'em.

Once more we must thank our friend Graham Walker for "Road Tests Recalled" and a copy of "Motor Cycling Manual." The latter, I think I am right in saying, is the only book of its kind in IV B, and if, and when, you get hold of it, please treat it carefully.

When any of the Club's books come to your hut you can greatly help our circulation manager, Alan Vidow, by passing on to all other club members in the hut. Please do not leave the books idle, they must have the maximum use it is possible to give them.

All books will circulate the huts in strict rotation, so have patience, you will eventually read them. Please remember, there are more than one hundred others to read the books after you — so treat them with consideration.

Do you know!

Wear on Road Surface

The Ministry of Transport tests at Harmondsworth have shown that wear on a concrete road made with gravel aggregate, is almost negligible, being at the rate of one inch in 220 years on a 20 foot carriageway carrying over 16,000 tons of traffic per day.

Tyre Wear

That the German International "Six Days" Trial teams completely changed their tyres at the conclusion of each day's riding. This was due to the use of home produced "rubber." Our own official teams stated that they could ride even another duplicate "Six Days", and without anxiety.

Ersatz

That for such articles as petrol pipes, pump diaphragms, etc., the artificial rubber (developed during the present hostilities) is far superior to the natural rubber.

Big End Bearings

That progressive manufacturers are breaking away from convention, an example is the split cap, plain big end bearings. (Car type).

Hints & Tips

SPRING LINK TRACING
Made easy

Delay is often exper-ienced when chang-ing or repairing motor cycle chains. This is caused through a layer of grease covering the spring link and thus making it similar to the roller links. A racing dodge can be easily copied and will eliminate all future troubles.

Pick out the spring link, clean it thor-oughly so as to remove all grease, and then coat it with a bright paint (red, green, etc.). Rapid identification will result; an occasional wipe will keep it "obvious."

Refitting Chains

Frequently the nov-ice motor cyclist is seen struggling to fit the spring clip into the two chain ends, when refitting his chains. He no doubt fervently wishes for an-other pair of hands.

The mistake is made by keeping the two ends tensioned in <u>between</u> both sprockets (the same applies to both chains). The obvious meth-od then is to thread the chain on to one sprocket, so that the two ends meet somewhere con-venient on the other sprocket. The teeth on the sprockets hold the chain in place

For those who Hibernate

The real enthusiast shudders when asked if he is "laying-up" the machine for winter; (and most probably considers the remark a form of slight upon his manliness.)

But the matter must be faced up to — there is a percentage of us who have (either from economy — or wet and cold funk) to "dry-dock" the model. It is also readily accepted that certain precautions should be taken to ensure that a *motor cycle* is ready for the next riding season, and not a heap of rusty junk.

Perhaps the first move in the laying-up process should be the securing of a dry shed (emphasis on the dry) with a board floor prefered.

Remove the battery and either wash it out and store, or send to a service station for recharging, (repeat several times through the winter.) Next thoroughly wash the machine, (a weak hosing to soak any mud through, then a sponge and hose applied intelligently). Thoroughly dry, and the machine is advanced a little in the laying-up process. Follow on by draining the petrol tank, ensuring that there is no deposit of dirt left in the corners and filters (it will probably pay to take the tank off to clean): the oil tank should follow, being particularly painstaking in flushing the filter as well as the tank; this also applies to the sump and gearbox (sludge has a nasty habit of solidifying). Probably the best way is to drain and swill through with petrol and then, after allowing vapourisation — flush through with light oil.

Next, remove all chains, drop them into a paraffin oil bath — give them a chance to soak and then scrub them well with a stiff brush; swing them about briskly to throw off any surplus paraffin and then store them

in lubricating oil. The engine, gearbox, sprockets, etc., should be scrubbed off with paraffin and thoroughly dried.

One of the most important details is the re-packing of all bearings and lubricating points with good grease (by means of a pressure gun). Pump grease in until all the old, dirty grease has oozed out and fresh new grease can be observed.

Smear all electrical contact points with vaseline, taking care not to get any on parts of the wiring harness; bulbs should be put away in their boxes.

The next task is to smear all the enamel-ed and plated parts of the model with a good grease: for a painstaking rider who has the necessary time on hand the tyres and inner tubes will receive special attention. Remove the outer covers, give the inner tubes a good wash in warm soapy water, keeping them slightly inflated, dry thoroughly and dust liberally with french chalk. A minute examination of the outer cover should take place for cuts, grit, etc. Replace tube and outer cover and inflate slightly; raise the model on its stands (front and rear) or if a front stand is not fitted then a wooden box under the crankcase will suit. Cover the model with a dust-sheet or old raincoats and the winter hibernation period will not harm "the old moke", rather,

will find it panting eagerly when Spring comes back.

If the reader happens to be an enthusiast— who desires to overhaul his machine during the laying-up period, then obviously, as he cleans and flushes, etc., he will be taking note of all minor as well as major adjustments and replacements. It is doubtful whether a better means of spending a winter season exists, but of course only the true enthusiast thinks this way.

To conclude this article a good tip for long period storing has come to mind. Just this— completely strip the machine, clean thoroughly— then drop the lot in a tub of oil. (It's been done! Exclude soft goods).

An Advertising offer

Are you in business? If so, perhaps we can help you. We take this opportunity to offer the "Flywheel" advertising pages to members desirous of making their business better known. If you wish to avail yourself of this opportunity, then contact A.H.Pill, Hut 47A.

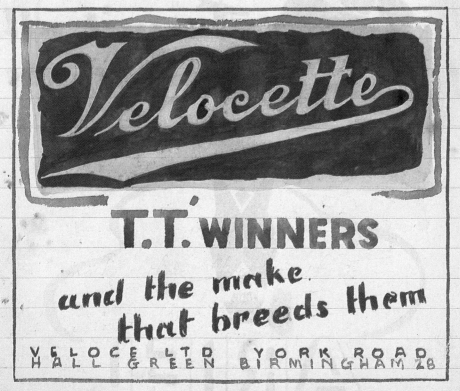

Velocette

T.T. WINNERS

and the make that breeds them

VELOCE LTD YORK ROAD
HALL GREEN BIRMINGHAM 28

FLYWHEEL STAFF ●● P.C. HARRINGTON-JOHNSON ● A.H. PILL
T. RODGER ● W. STOBBS ● D. MUMFORD ● A. VIDOW ●

Contents

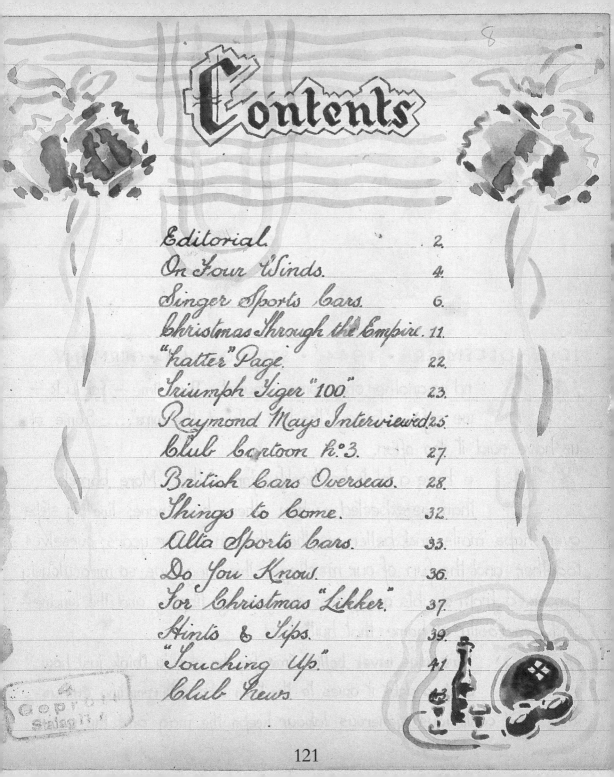

The FLYWHEEL

XMAS NUMBER

"KEEPS THE WORKS GOING ROUND ON THE IDLE STROKES"

NO·8 DECEMBER · 1944 · STALAG IV B · GERMANY

And so another one comes round. This time — for luck — we refuse to say "the last behind the wire".... Some of us have said it too often.

We have a lot to be thankful for, at that. More parcels than we expected — when others have none; two big steps over; hope, mails and better weather than in earlier years; ourselves together, and the fun of our meetings; this magazine so miraculously produced from doubts and fears; our growing library and the kindness and generosity at home that built it....

There was never better time for the club to think just how deep a debt it owes to the team whose unremitting enthusiasm and continuous generous labour keeps the mag. and the supplement going. Some of us realise just how much work, time and care it takes.

So to these stout fellows, I — as one of you who enjoy as you do this, their work — will try to express our inadequate thanks and appreciation.

Gentlemen — "and your foot on the table" —

Arthur Pill, 'Moggy' Rodger, Bill Stobbs, Bob Mumford, Allan Vidow, Bill Trevvett, Roy Clackett — and Uncle Graham Walker. God Bless 'em!

At other Xmases, in years to be, far from these windy flats by the sluggish Elbe — let us look back with gratitude to our days together here — rembering how that, despite short rations, cold, overcrowding, uncertain parcels and erratic mail, we yet managed to get together in a warm fellowship — united by the comradeship of The Game.

Editor

Greetings
To all Club Members
From the Committee.
And may the next one be — At Home

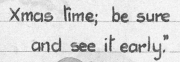

By the time some of you read this you will already have seen and, I trust, read this month's "Flywheel" Supplement, but for those members who are early on the circulation list all I can say is "This month's issue contains a surprise, as pleasant as one usually receives at Xmas time; be sure and see it early."

The illustrations and description, of the "secret" leaves no one in any doubt whatsoever as to how our new models will look and perform, and all true motorcyclists, I feel sure, will experience a thrill equal, almost, to their first ride, that will give the 'works' an extra little bit of urge on this, the idle stroke.

Prior to September 1939 very few of us had ever seen, or even heard, of the 'Auto-Scooter,' the little 'scooter' (one can hardly call it a motorcycle) which was to be found in the U.S.A. and it was not until May '41 that I actually

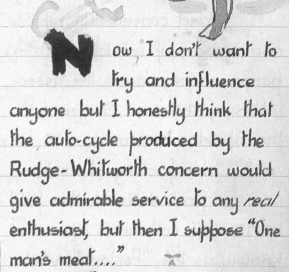

saw one – in the Middle East. The first thing that struck me was its flamboyant colour – orange; next, the wheels, I thought were far too small and the engine, enclosed as it was, could not possibly operate; but one of our latest members, newly arrived from the U.K., states that he did quite a lot of 'scooting' on one of these tiny 'heroes', including a run of 40 miles, and was so impressed that he is considering building himself a weatherproof job for use as a runabout, riding to work the whole year round, etc. (lightness in weight, tax, petrol and easy maintenance being the object.)

Winds

Now, I don't want to try and influence anyone but I honestly think that the auto-cycle produced by the Rudge-Whitworth concern would give admirable service to any *real* enthusiast, but then I suppose "One man's meat...."

They have great possibilities, these little chaps. Give it thought!

Sports Cars

BY P. C. HARRINGTON-JOHNSON

Sterling value for money and consistently reliable and good – if not top-notch – performance, mark the association of the name Singer with the sports car world.

The factory (I think) first entered this field in 1926-7 with an 8 h.p. car known as the "Porlock." While I cannot be sure that this *was* the first sports model of this old house – those years were the boom ones for motor sport and saw the rise of the sports light car to popularity, and it seems unlikely that the "Porlock" was *not* "Singer Sports Nº1." It had a 4-cyl. 850 c.c., o.h.c.

(chain), motor with inclined valves (ports all on one side of the head), a three speed long-lever ball-change gear box, wire wheels of bolt-on pattern, cable brakes, magneto, single carburettor, and a neat slipper-type two seater open body with a distinctive "duck's" tail.

Well tuned, the car had a ferocious exhaust note and would do just over 70, but as the crankshaft was two-bearing and big-ends splash oiled, life at this speed was about ¼ mile. In normal user however, the engines were very long lived. The "Porlock" earned fame for itself by one hundred

successive ascents of the Welsh "terror hill" Bwlch-y-Groes.

In 1932 Singers produced another car — the Nine Sports. This had the justly famous 972 c.c. o.h.c. engine with four cylinders, four speeds and Lockheed brakes and a two seater sports body of stub-tailed, valanced-side type.

By the end of the year the famous 'Le Mans' model was on sale, incorporating the lessons learned in this French venture.

Five different "Le Mans" models came out in the next four years. Best known was the two seater open "9", with a 972 c.c., 4-cyl., o.h.c., engine. An "International Formula 2/4 seater"

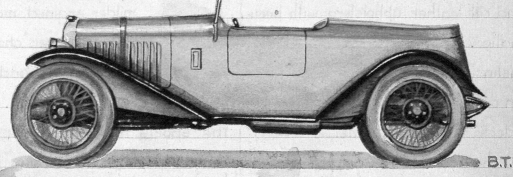

B.T.

In 1933 a car with this engine and a touring body was run in the 24 hour Grand Prix d' Endurance at Le Mans, the back seats being replaced by a huge petrol tank.

body of aluminium was used, with two doors and a big rear tank fitted with chrome wire-mesh stone guards, cycle-type mud-guards and a flared scuttle, a remote-change to the four speed

synchro gearbox, finned sump (of alloy), five inch rev. meter and "clock", and quick fillers, were standard. The detail specification was lavish and of first rate make. Double Hartford "shockers" all round, finned Lockheed brake drums, Rudge racing hubs and wire wheels, Smith-Jaeger instruments, spring spoke steering wheel, and all leather upholstery with pneumatic cushions were standard. Distinctive was the heavy chrome on all plated parts and the metal "deck" under the bonnet to which all the tools were strapped or clipped. Twin S.U. or Solex carburettors were fitted, the ports being on opposite sides of the head, and the plugs were "pocketed." Cars of this type could do 80-85 in top, nearly 80 in third, and their unusually high ground clearance and wonderfully smooth pulling of the two-bearing engine at low speeds made them excellent and renowned trials cars. The firm took up racing but with indifferent success. For its size, the "Le Mans" 9 was smart, long-lived, tough and nippy—a joy to possess.

A milder engined model with a longer chassis and four seater touring and saloon bodies was made. All the sports trimmings were retained and maximum was just over 70. miles per hour.

Contemplation

About 1936-37 a faster two seater model with a more highly tuned engine fitted

B.T.

with a Scintilla Vertex magneto, costing £15 extra, was introduced, and by 1937-38 a racing model with a guaranteed top speed of 90 m.p.h. was on sale for £525. This car had a streamlined point-tailed two seater body, cycle-type guards, 14 gallon tank with twin fillers and headlamps fitted to struts on the dumbirons. It was the swan song of the "Le Mans" type. Three cars — one driven by Stanley Barnes, another by S.C.H. Davis — famous racing editor of "The Autocar"— and the third by D. Clayton Wright were

entered for the T.T. at Ards. A faulty billet of steel had been used for the steering tie rods of all three, and first one, and then a second car, went out of control and crashed at speed with broken steering on successive laps. The third car, though going well, was withdrawn.

In 1934 a 1½ litre "Le Mans" two seater came out. To look at — and in fact — a "grown-up" 9, it was

run at Le Mans that year with a 1,496 c.c. 6-cylinder chain-driven single o.h.c. The model was later a consistent trials performer, driven by Barnes. About this time a 6-cylinder 4-speed 2-carburettor sports o.h.c. saloon was introduced — but little is known of the type, which did not last long on the market.

At the end of 1937 the famous "Le Mans" type was discontinued, and racing abandoned — though a team of the streamlined "9's" were maintained privately for a time by the Barnes Brothers.

In 1939 a sports version of the 9 h.p. "Bantam" was produced with a bored-out 1,021 c.c. 4-cyl. engine, 3 bearing crankshaft, chain-driven o.h. camshaft of special type, single S.U. carburettor and three speed synchro. gearbox, with long-lever change. Girling brakes, Armstrong hydraulic progressive-acting "shockers," steel disc wheels and under-slung back axle were standard and an attractive open four seater body of aluminium with sorbo and leather seats and with a flared scuttle, sprung spoke wheel and the traditional tool "deck" were other popular fittings. Sliding glass side curtains cost £2. 10s. 0d. extra. The model was known as the

Continued on Page 26

Preparation

CHRISTMAS
Through The Empire

Christmas, the season of "peace on earth, goodwill towards men," is, without doubt, the highlight of British family life and, from start to finish, is the period of hustle, bustle and excitement. The shops, which are trimmed long before the 24th., must be visited by all and sundry. The children must pay a visit to Santa Claus (always placed in such a spot that you just cannot resist the bright lights of the various departments before reaching him) and by the time one gets home much more has been spent than was intended.

But in spite of all the pleas to "shop early and avoid the rush" Xmas Eve is always the busiest time of the year. The shops remain open indefinitely and even as late as 11 p.m. the long rows of turkeys are still being reinforced. All good things come to an end, however, and finally an ex-

pectant hush settles upon the sleeping city, town or village. The children, for once, were ready for bed long before it was time, because they realise that the last few hours before diving into the tightly packed stocking, pass quicker in sleep.

Long before it is light the children are awake and happy cries can be heard from all direct- ions, but, even so they are usually preceeded by the heroes from the Highway's Department, who, in bad wea- ther, must make the roads fit for the happy throng that will soon be using them.

By 9.30 breakfast is over, Mum and Sis are busy getting the dinner ready and Dad has hurried away to the annual "Derby." Jim, on his motorbike, has other ways of spending Xmas morning. His club organises a run into the country to "build up an appetite" for an assault upon the turkey, pork, potatoes, sprouts, apple sauce and Xmas Pud, etc.. Some clubs make a habit of collecting holly and mistletoe (in lieu of the 'Yule' log), thereby combining pleas- ure present, with pleasure future, for after a glorious dinner everyone has a party to go to and a sprig of mistle- toe can be very useful during

Exhilaration

the fun which follows the sumptuous tea....

When one struggles home in the early hours of the morning (humming "Where, oh where do I live?")

sounds of revelry can still be heard en route. And so to bed, to repeat the performance the next day when the motto is "Eat, drink and be merry, for tomorrow — we must work."

T. Swallow

CANADA
by V. S. Hawkes

The festive season in Canada must find cars thoroughly "winterized" against the severe weather. A car must be able to cope with conditions of freezing sleet right down to driving blizzards, at 40° below. We use anti-freeze that will stand 50° below zero and thin oil in the crank-case of a grade 10 S.A.E.

To guarantee good visibility, storm windows with ⅟₁₆" clearance on all glass should be attached; this prevents frosting — so dangerous to winter motoring. To keep our engines warm and also to keep driving snow from shorting the spark plugs the bonnet is covered with a thick waterproof blanket and shutters are attached to the front of the radiator. You can well imagine that in bucking against a 40 m.p.h. wind in a freezing temperature well

below zero, a small opening of the radiator shutters is ample for cooling the engine.

For passenger comfort there are several types of heaters, the most popular is similar to a radiator, placed under the dashboard, which keeps the inside at about 55° while the car is in motion. A set of chains, shovel and a tow-cable just about completes the necessities for driving in Canada's frigid zones.

Many people on Boxing Day motor out to their country cabin in the woods for a little hunting, or to the winter-sports resorts in the mountains. Others fill everything, except the gas tank and crank-case, with booze,

and make the rounds of friends, but I believe the most popular festive pastime is tobogganing or skiing — towed behind the car.

You would be thrilled to sit on a nice long toboggan with a controllable rope around the bumper of a car, skimming along a smooth surfaced, snow covered road at about 40 m.p.h. It's dangerous if the driver is at all reckless but with experienced drivers it is such fun — it's almost "low flying" at its best. Needless to say one must be very warmly dressed.

In skiing behind a car there are always country lakes for the best conditions. My favourite lake was about 14 miles long and one mile wide. As a rule it had a thick, even surface of ice, with two or three inches of powdery snow, just ideal for skiing. Even if you are adequately dressed one length at high speed is about the limit for comfort. Once your car gets under way it is quite possible to reach 60 or 70 m.p.h; the snow flies, as in a driving blizzard, behind the speeding wheels, so you must row at an angle or else in a few hundred yards you'd look like a speeding snowman. A few smartly negotiated curves increases the pleasure, and as in other countries, our cars come in handy in making the rounds of friends in Yuletide feast and frolic.

AUSTRALIA
by J. Edwards

With Christmas coming at a more congenial time of the year, the festive season is celebrated in an altogether different manner to that of the colder climes.

The suggestion that we go for a surf would be viewed with alarm in latitudes such as this, but to an Aussie it is the usual thing to do. Surfing is the most popular way of spending the holidays, and the beaches are crowded from daylight till late at night with people absorbing

Vitamin "D" and changing colour through pretty pink to deep brown.

A big majority of the population "go somewhere" during Xmas, so you find people going up the coast, down the coast, to the country or from the country. Some have family re-unions, others move out to avoid them, some even go hiking.

M uch petrol and oil is burnt up and vehicles of all nationalities either glide by with a swish of their tails, a bang, spit and protest surrounded with a blue haze, or are propelled by their occupants along the highways, main roads and lesser roads, at various speeds.

W hile brother motorists in other countries are de-icing and dosing the "bug" with anti-freezing dope, our "pride and joy" is converting water to steam in no uncertain manner— and not another drop for fifty miles.

O wing to the liquor laws of certain states purchases must be made before 6. p.m. on Xmas eve—or any other eve. In practice this means that by the time the "mid-lower" and "overload" tanks have been filled, (gathered up tomorrow's quarts) it is 11.59 p.m. and Christmas has arrived once more. The

Oscillation

national drink never changes, not even for Xmas, but to compensate for this apparent lack of imagination, more is consumed.

Tradition dies hard and with the temperature clocking around the 100 mark or over, the Christmas feast of the Old Country is prepared and eaten, for what would Xmas be without turkey and the pudding?

Local motor cycle and car clubs take advantage of the holidays to hold trials, hill climbs, rallies or just plain parties. At one time the Australian Speedway Championships were held in Sydney — these activities conclude our Christmas festivities — but not this year.

NEW ZEALAND

by Kiwi Curtis

While we shiver under the grey skies of the northern winter New Zealanders will be basking in the bright sunshine of mid-summer.

Just what civvy petrol ration, if any, is in force "down under" we do not know, but presuming there is one — at least for the holidays — N.Z. motorists will be able to pack some extensive travelling into the weekend. Most people will be free from 11 p.m. Christmas eve, over Sunday, Monday and Tuesday.

Lucky ones in some professions and trades will have longer.

Due to the difference in seasons between the two hemispheres, the average New Zealander does not "go for" the Yule Log, mistletoe, big fire and plum pudding of the traditional English Xmas. His ideas run to the beaches and beer, ice cream and fruit salad and because nearly every N.Z. family own a car a big proportion of families are away from home for the festive season, often making a run on Xmas Eve to wherever they have elected to spend Christmas day.

As a result, beaches and scenic resorts are crowded with visitors over the holidays. Bags of sports events are held on Boxing Day, hotels and motor camps everywhere are packed with people. The motor camp is a feature of every place with 1,000 - 1,500 population — or more. People book sites at the camps weeks before the holidays and the casual camper who drifts into a camp on Xmas Eve or Day, has just about "had his time".

Most camping motorists have their own caravans or tents, but some camps are elaborately fitted up with cabins which may be hired. All camps have cooking, washing, eating and sanitary conveniences.

Mortification   PM

Cooking is done on electric hot-plates or gas rings, on the penny-slot system. Hot and cold showers are available at most camps. The charge is 1s. 0d. to 2s. 6d. per day according to the facilities provided. There is great camaraderie at the camps and the newcomer is always given a friendly hand, if he wants it.

So the motorists of the south will be on the road these holidays — if petrol permits; searching out their favourite spots, swimming, boating, playing golf and tennis, fluttering a few "quid" on the "mokes" and knocking back the good old tonsil tonic, while we.... but why bring that up?

SOUTH AFRICA
by J. Will

Christmas in South Africa means the end of the harvesting season and mid-summer, so everybody who can manage it, knocks off from work to flock down to the coast or to one of the many inland holiday resorts, where there is usually a swimming bath or river, where it is possible to cool off before settling down to iced drinks and cold lunches.

Xmas also brings a motor gymkhana for the enthusiasts - held on Boxing

Day. For New Year's Day we have the biggest motoring events of the year. The South African Handicap to warm up on, and then the S.A. Grand Prix — both run on the Prince George Circuit, which is in East London, a port for the Cape Province. People go there from all over the Union, covering great distances in pretty short times to see some of the world's best drivers at work, pitting their skill and machines against each other.

Among the British and Continental drivers were to be seen, Earl Howe and the late Dick Seaman in their E.R.A.'s, Rosemeyer in his Auto Union, and Villaresi in the Maserati. From South Africa, "Mario" and Steve Cabbini in their Maseratis, Roderick in his Alfa Romeo, the late Roy Hesketh with his M.G. and many others could be seen taking part in the two races.

Accomodation being very difficult to procure, it is a common sight to see thousands of people camping alongside the track — which follows the coast. I usually leave home the evening before the race, and go straight into one of the car parks on the track, see the racing and return home the same night, covering a total distance of 640 miles, very tired but happy.

As for next Xmas — home? — let's hope so!

Natter Page

A 'washouse' is hardly the chummiest choice for a club room and consequently does not allow lengthy get-together conversations, or 'experience swapping' either. There is invariably a show going in full swing, or some other distraction in the attached bungalow. In order to surmount these inconveniences we have decided to give an 'official welcome', through the "Flywheel", to all new members, also to make it known whether or not they desire to 'enter into conversation' upon any pet machine or technical matter. If you wish to be enlightened upon any motoring enquiry — just put it up to us — our club 'No. 9 hats' will probably be able to help.

May all new members pass as many happy and interesting hours with their peace time hobby as the remainder of the club has. Let's hope that soon we will turn theory into practice and make up some of our lost motoring mileage.

R. Pick 49A. wishes contact with practical 'Specials' builders (Hush-Hush)

L. Rake. 24A wishes to contact Bedford drivers, or owners.

I. Ledingham requires contact with practical caravan builder. (60B)

B. May. 26B. requires contact with metal worker, or 'gen' on plastics.

D. Davies looks for Ariel 'SquareFour' and "chair" experience.

TRIUMP

"**A** thing of beauty is a joy for ever" — this old phrase very aptly, in my way of thinking, sums up the "Tiger 100". Developed from the original Triumph Vertical Twin, it makes a very attractive proposition for the idealist, for surely a machine of this calibre should not be allowed even *near* any of the "ham-fisted" rag and bob-tail.

This 500 c.c. o.h.v. twin immediately presents a picture of "rightness", the controls well placed, handlebars of natural bend, a fine degree of adjustability with footrests, saddle, 'bars etc.. These details *are* important — and yet so often neglected, thus spoiling good machines.

First-kick starting is a reality — not a sales slogan, cold weather requires a couple of sucking-in strokes to ensure an instant response. Mag. cut-out control is by button mounted on the handlebars. The smooth purr of a well-balanced engine comes pleasingly from

large capped megaphones, the

Tiger

ends of which are easily detachable for racing purposes.

A feature of the machine which makes itself apparent early on is the ratchet twistgrip — a Triumph patent. The possibility

D. Mumford.

of the ratchet slipping is very

slight, and according to those in authority, is estimated at 1,000,000,000 to 1, much safer than the orthodox in fact. A too heavy slice of throttle combined with a banged-out clutch will make the front wheel rise in no uncertain manner — that should indicate that "100" has plenty of "umph". Speeds through the gears are terrific and the maker's claim of 100 per is no idle one, but most riders fight shy before that magic figure is reached.

To turn to the other end of the scale, a top-gear performance of 16 m.p.h, with ignition fully advanced,

CONTINUED ON P.26

Raymond Mays INTERVIEWED by Nemo

"**I** really have no idea how I shall fare after this long enforced absence from the game," quoth Raymond Mays to "yours truly" during a conversation the other day.

It had come to pass that I, an ardent Mays and E.R.A. fan, was stationed in the town of B-----, and, upon learning of the great man's presence there, made haste to become known to him.

After viewing the M.C.T. (Mays Collection of Trophies) — three rooms full — and mentally comparing them with my own four inscribed egg cups, the talk naturally turned to post-war racing.

"**C**elebrated my 43rd. birthday not so long ago," said Ray, "and that made me think more than ever that it's about time I stood down for some young blood." The twinkle in his eyes assured me that these words were spoken in jest. This assurance was borne out as Mays, continuing, said. "In my opinion though, no race driver reaches his prime before the age of thirty. With regard to my own case, I was 35 before my driving satisfied me."

Of his plans for E.R.A.s "later on," Mr. Mays was very non-committal. "But," he hastened to inform me, "although I myself have been resting, my

mind hasn't, and rest assured that I'll have something ready for the first post-war Donnington meeting."

The famous 1½ litre is lying in the garage adjoining the Mays' residence, whilst a 2 litre engine, partly dismembered, rests on a nearby workbench.

Here's hoping then, that it won't be long before once more we'll be standing at Melbourne corner watching Mays slide round in his inimitable manner, with the pack in a snarling bunch at his heels.

SINGER SPORTS CONTINUED

"Roadster," cost £169. 10s. and in tuned form can do 75 m.p.h. The good clearance made it useful in the Dominions and a larger 10-12 h.p. chassis was made specially for Australian use. It was a most likeable and friendly little sporting car.

TIGER "100" CONTINUED

must be experienced in order to appreciate it, and then to accelerate away from most things on two or four wheels. To quote a "best" touring speed would be impossible, the running throughout the "scale" being of such a high order.

The gearbox proved sweet in action, following normal Triumph practice of

CONCLUDED ON P. 40

Club Cartoon No 3

BRITISH CARS OVERSEAS

by KIWI

It should be apparent even to the casual student of economics that for Britain to have a good standard of living after the war her export trade must be built up to, and maintained at, a high level. Motor vehicles should be one of the main exports.

Pre-war, motor exports ranked high on the export list but could have been boosted to a much greater degree had there been more co-operation between industry and government and had the vehicles been more suited to the conditions under which they were operated overseas. British motor cycles, on the basis of value for money, performance and reliability were ahead of all rivals and British high speed, light weight Diesels are unmatched by any foreign product—so that trucks fitted with these motors should sell well overseas. The British car is a horse of a different colour — that is, the mass production job such as the Austin, Morris, Standard, Vauxhall, Hillman and British Ford.

Overseas conditions are vastly different

from English and criticisms commonly made of British cars by Dominion and Colonial owners are: Power-weight ratio too low, springing too hard, low ground clearance, motors insufficiently cooled, wear and tear excessive (due to hard driving of small bore motors with long stroke and high piston speeds). That these cars are reasonably suited to British conditions is no consolation to the car buyer overseas. He may be patriotically-minded enough to want to buy a British car but no working man can afford to study patriotism alone when spending £300 to £400 on a car. In N.Z., with which the writer is most acquaint-

ed, an Austin 12 cost £335 in 1939. An American Ford V8 or Chevrolet could be bought at the same price despite the big preferential tariff in favour of the Austin. The only advantage of the British car was its better m.p.g. In all other aspects of performance it was outclassed by the American car which was also entirely suited to N.Z. conditions whereas the British car was not.

Yet British car exports to the Dominions (except Canada which has its branch factories building American cars in Canada) increased appreciably over the seven years before the war. This was achieved under hot house conditions—not on merit—

because at the Empire tariff conference at Ottawa in 1932 inter-Empire tariffs were rearranged as between Britain and the Dominions. These tariffs were designed to stop unlimited exploitation of Empire markets by exporters in foreign countries which maintained high tariffs to prevent Empire products from being sold competitively in those countries. Actually the tariffs were aimed mainly at the United States which from 1918 on had dumped steadily increasing quantities of exports in the Empire but refused to take from Empire in exchange and demanded gold in payment.

After 1932 N.Z. rearranged import duties to give substantial preference to United Kingdom products first, to Empire products second, with foreign third. Prior to 1932 an Austin "7" cost more than the cheaper American cars with big engines and comfortable riding (for those days). Mighty few Austins were sold but the new tariff rates raised the prices of American cars till they became dearer than British "sevens" and "tens" and the same price as "twelves". In the bigger sizes, however, British jobs were still far dearer than the American quality cars. In the period 1938-39 Britain supplied nearly 60% of N.Z.'s motor vehicle imports, over 25% came from Canada, 10% direct from the United States and the small balance from Germany and Italy.

British cars also increased sales in other overseas markets due to tariff preferences, or because by absorbing exports from certain foreign countries Britain could demand that such countries take a fair volume of British goods in exchange. There is a limit to the volume of British goods that can be forced on overseas markets by these methods and it is not enough for Britain to barter exports against imports. She needs an export balance and it will need to be a big balance in post war years to pay for the war and give the higher standard of living Britain wants to achieve.

The solution is for Britain to make goods that will sell overseas on their merits. There are over 70,000,000 Europeans alone in the Empire, with only a little over half of them in the U.K. It is not good business practice to make goods suitable for U.K. conditions only and try to sell the same goods to the balance of potential buyers on a take-it-or-leave-it basis. The buyers are too inclined to leave it.

The British horse power tax, which compels the use of small engines in chassis too heavy for them, is the chief trouble. If it were scrapped, British makers could build cars suited to overseas conditions. Such cars should have a

CONTINUED P. 42

Things to come

Festive season brings no new attraction,
Impatience grows through lack of action.
Members yearn to take the road once more,
In scrambles, trials or on a country tour.

While fat old men gaze smugly from their cars,
Enthusiasts are frozen to the bars.
But worse — the Morgan, little in-between,
With ice-bound driver fixed behind the screen

All these are represented in the club,
Each one prepared to give or take a snub,
Supporting Rudge or Frazer-Nash until
The lights go out and they surmount the sill.

Soon, when Tommy's spud-packed pouch is bulging,
Saner folk indoors are all indulging.
Then wheels will spin under the M.M.C.
In better times around the Christmas Tree.

P.J. Bemrose

HALT

ALTA

A New Sports Car

by Frank Street

Introduced only a few years before the present war, this range of cars is noteworthy in having high performance and being of fine construction, virtually handmade.

Made by the Alta Car and Engineering Co., of Surbiton, under the direction of Mr. Geoffrey Taylor, the three engine sizes in normal production are basically similar; the capacities are 1,100 ccs., 1½ litres and 2 litres, blown and unblown, fitted to two-seater sports and monoposto racing cars. The latter may be had with normal or independent suspension. All have 4-cyl. motors.

• 1100 Models •

The following features are common to all types: Swept volume of 1,074 c.cs, R.A.C. rating 9 h.p., yearly tax £6. 15s. (pre-war), £11. 5s. (present). Alloy linered block, alloy head, twin overhead camshafts, three bearing crankshaft, pump and fan cooling, forced feed lubrication (high pressure to mains and big ends, subsidiary to timing gears, camshafts etc.) S.U. carb(s)., ignition — magneto or coil, four speed pre-selective gearbox, steering wheel control, wheelbase 8'0" or 8'6". and very low ground clearance.

The sports range consisted of two-seater and two-seater competition cars priced at £398. They were unblown and developed 50 b.h.p. at 6,000 r.p.m. Top 108 m.p.h., third 80/85, consumption 22 m.p.g. price £498.

The 1,074 c.c. racing car, costing £850, will do 120 m.p.h. and, with normal suspension, weighs 11¼ cwt.

speed 85 m.p.h, consumption 30/35 m.p.g. These types were discontinued in 1938.

The supercharged sports version is remarkable in having the greatest power output, per litre, of any production model, viz. 107 b.h.p at 6,000 r.p.m. Speed on top is

Fuel consumption is 7 m.p.g.

1½ Litre Models

4 cylinder, 1488 c.cs. capacity, R.A.C. rating 12 h.p. Tax £9 (pre-war) £15 at (present). Engine details as in 1100 c.c. models. The U/S sports engine develops 75 b.h.p. at 5,500 r.p.m., consumption 28 m.p.g.

Speed 95 m.p.h., price £498. The addition of a blower increases the b.h.p. to 130 at the same peak r.p.m., the top speed to 112 m.p.h. and the price to £598, consumption 20 m.p.g.

The 1,500 c.c racing jobs may be had with normal or independent wheel suspension. The latter is worthy of special attention, for, in the hands of G. Abecassis such a car put up very creditable performances, even against works E.R.A.s and the '1,500' Maseratis. Specification included nitrided nitralloy crankshaft, water cooled main bearings, separate oil cooler, tubular chassis of welded construction and suspension by transverse torsion bars with trailing arms at the front and leading arms at the rear end. The power output was about 210 b.h.p. at 6,800 r.p.m. (22 lbs per sq.in. supercharge) maximum speed — 165 m.p.h., at the cost of £1,200.

• 2 Litre Models •

Capacity 1980 c.cs. rated at 15 h.p. Details as for 1,100 c.c.

The unblown two-seater develops 90 b.h.p at 5,000 r.p.m. and has a top speed of 100 m.p.h. consumption 25 m.p.g. The supercharged version* out 150 b.h.p, sufficient for a speed of 120 m.p.h., the highest of any sports car. Petrol consumption is 18 m.p.g. and the prices the same as the 1,500 c.c. jobs. (*Ommission - gives)

Do you know

That Great Britain's oil problem has been solved to a large extent? In recent months oil has been discovered in Cumberland, the estimation for quantity is that sufficient has been located to last us for the next fifty years. The presence of oil-bearing shale had been known for several years, but the quantity has hitherto been insufficient to allow economical production to take place.

Our supply is ensured for half a century and it is pretty certain that in this time a new fuel — or method of propulsion — will have been developed.

That another vertical twin-cylindered motor cycle has appeared in production — making the fourth vertical twin in the Triumph range? It is a 500 cc. side-valve, touring, utility model, the valve gear being mounted "fore and aft" the block. Approximate price will be £70.

That torsion bar springing has been incorporated in a hush-hush model from the Vincent H.R.D. works? We are told that if an oblong box with a torsion bar protruding from each end and attached to two wheels can be imagined — well, that's it. Presumably a saddle and handlebars, etc, are also fitted…!

Fo' "CHRISTMAS" Likker

BY "NEMO"

Christmas, '42! What a joint, we thought, away out in the wilds of Tunisia, somewhere in front of Beja.

I felt a trifle sorry for the boys, in the usual Don R manner; after all, I was on the move all the time and didn't have to stick around the dilapidated farmhouse — a forward position — all day.

Mid-morning came, and with it a run to the French Commandos who were in position about 20 kilos. off. An exceptionally wet and muddy journey ensued, but one which was, nevertheless, thoroughly enjoyable, fully half the distance being covered standing on the rests.

Whilst awaiting a reply, one of the Frenchmen — a brother enthusiast — admired the 350 Ariel and mentioned that it was the very thing he required to go for the Christmas wine. At the mention of the magic word "Muscatel," my ears pricked up, and upon enquiring where it was to be obtained, was informed that the famous monastery of Thibar was only a matter of 25 to 30 kilos away.

All corners on the way back were taken at breakneck speed, and my Section Officer, when informed of the fact that " le meilleur Muscat" could be had in quantity

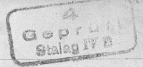
near at hand, gave me his bless-
ing plus four 2-Gallon water
cans.

Bosom pal "Micky"
scrounged a couple
of pieces of rope, and five minutes
later we set off, each with two cans
suspended around our necks. For
those who don't know, Thibar Monastery lies on the top of a mountain,
and it is reached by one solitary
mountain track which skirts, a
trifle precariously at times, yawn-
ing chasms and deep gorges. This
was more than I'd bargained for,
but the ascent was successfully
accomplished, much to my surprise
—and Micky's.

"**A**vez-vous....?" I began,
addressing the first
monk I saw. "Whit d'ye want", he
enquired with a marked Glasgow

accent. I was "shaken rigid" until it
was explained to me that the
monks here come from all walks of
life and from all over the world.
Eventually receiving the "vin", the
most thrilling ride I have ever experienced commenced.

I should here, I think,
explain that by this
time dusk was rapidly approaching,
and this, together with a stinging
rain and a vicious biting cross
wind, made both Micky and myself a trifle apprehensive of the
descent of the mountain.

How I ever managed
to stay with the
machine the whole way down
surprises me more today than
it actually did at the time, but
suffice to say that the wine
reached its destination about an

CONTINUED ON P. 40

HINTS & TIPS

Here is a sound tip for keeping dry shirt tails on long trips during winter. Procure a mother's or wife's rubber kitchen apron, wear it as such – underneath one's riding coat – and another chink in the armour is well sealed.

All-weather riders will find this easily made saddle-cover an invaluable accessory for their machine. Obtain a piece of waterproof canvas (or rexine, oilcloth, etc.,) about 18" square. also two ½" × ³⁄₁₆" nuts, bolts and washers, two small draper's hooks and about 12" of blind cord.

Get the female to shape the canvas to the saddle top, allowing about 2" lap all round, and sew the edges to prevent fraying. Next, drill two holes, to take the bolts, in the back vertical portion of the saddle, put the canvas in place, washer the head end of the bolts, push them through the holes, tighten the nuts and the back end is secure. Mark on the inside of the canvas the best place for sewing the small hooks – so as they can conveniently catch under the

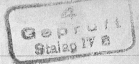

saddle-top edge, sew them on and the cover is complete.

When sitting on the saddle, the water-proof top is rolled up — until it is necessary to leave the the machine in the rain once more.

For CHRISTMAS "Likker" CONTINUED

hour and a half later. The absence of an exhaust valve lifter on the bike helped a helluva lot in the good time set up on the return journey. Some two hours later, thawed out by the heat of billet and the warm glow of "vin Muscat" in my guts, I joined the boys in a serious attempt to get properly 'blotto' and forget all about the war.

It is my firm conviction that any Tunisian who is given a motorbike will, in the course of a couple of years, be able to lick any of the British scramble 'cracks'. Yes, Haynes and Busty, too!

TIGER "100" CONTINUED

"one down" for bottom. Brakes were definite "stoppers" and have a smooth progressive action.

To sum up: the Triumph "Tiger 100", it is a machine of exemplary design, performance and finish and will prove a machine to help recapture some of our lost markets. "Yes — I am a "Tiger" 100 enthusiast!"

"Touching-up"

A few words regarding touching up paintwork which will probably aid the novice on future occasions and will probably save pounds over a period of years:—

Several types of 'paint' are available; both examples given are good and if instructions are followed a high-class finish should result. We will deal with brushing cellulose first.

Buy a good quality brand. Thoroughly clean the job — grease spots as well as dirt. Next, well damp the floor around the working space. And now to paint. Stir contents of tin thoroughly and then, using a good brush, apply the cellulose with a full, free flowing coat. Apply it quickly with as little brushing as possible.

Synthetic enamel must have very different treatment. Confine the painting to smaller areas than normal, apply the enamel sparingly so as to avoid runs, 'level off' with cross strokes and finally with vertical strokes, removing the surplus enamel by wiping the brush off on the edge of the tin after each stroke.

After each period of work clean the rim

of the paint tin with the brush, replace the lid and turn the tin upside down – to prevent a skin forming. A more experienced amateur will find one of the paint-spraying devices of greater service to him. A popular and inexpensive type utilises the car spare wheel. Only such jobs as mudguards can be completed on one inflation.

BRITISH CARS OVER SEAS continued

power-weight ratio comparable with the American. Springing should be softer. Dominion roads are either very good and permit high average speeds over long distances or are very poor, calling for hard slogging over rough surfaces and much heavy pulling on hard grades. Cooling should be more efficient because of higher temperatures overseas. Elimination of the horse power tax would let makers build big capacity motors, comparatively slow revving and capable of standing up to 50,000 to 60,000 miles of running without major repairs.

There are big markets overseas in which British cars should be pre-eminent. Given some enlightened assistance by the Government, the more progressive car manufacturers in Britain could double and treble overseas trade with benefit to the U.K. and to Dominion and Colonial motorists who would buy British because it's good – not because it's forced on them.

CLUB NEWS

If you have any secrets that you do not wish to be made public property I advise you not to let P.J. Bemrose, of the witty pen, or any of his satellites get hold of them. He is, I consider, entirely unscrupulous and I fear that our Ed. is not much better. Whilst we are on the subject, can't we do something about our artist? He does some headings and illustrations but really, Mr. Editor, can't you control him on the Cartoon Page?

Full marks are due to Geordie Elliott for his amusing tale of experiences in a "School For D.R's."

The Rudge v Triumph battle was again to the fore when 'Busty' Runyard gave his lecture on 'Scrambling with a Triumph.' He proved in no uncertain manner that the Triumph "was the world's best." In fact his 'boss' was only beaten once in a whole season and if this doesn't prove the superiority of the make I don't know what does. "What's that?" "The make that beat him on that occasion?— Oh well, it was an ancient Rudge, no good of course, just the usual old rattletrap."

Interested in model cars? — If so, contact A. H. Pill, 47A, with the view to forming a model car section of the Mühlburg Motor Club.

FERODO
Brake linings
MAKE MOTORING SAFE

FERODO

The **Motor** MANUALS

FOR INSTRUCTIONAL PURPOSES
THEY HAVE NO EQUAL

THE MOTOR MANUAL 5/-

THE MOTOR ELECTRICAL
MANUAL 3/6

HOW TO DRIVE A MOTOR
VEHICLE 3/6

TEMPLE PRESS
LTD.
BOWLING GREEN LANE LONDON E.C.1.

SERVICE BY SWALLOW

COAL MERCHANTS AND
HAULIERS

J. Swallow & Sons

BIRMINGHAM ROAD
OLDBURY
BIRMINGHAM

SERVICING BY
SWALLOW. BROS.
REPAIR SPECIALISTS
NEW & USED CARS
& MOTORCYCLE SALES.

45.

VAUXHALL

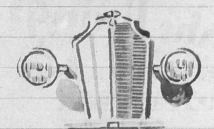

Used all over the World!

VAUXHALL MOTORS LIMITED LUTON BEDS.

Flywheel Staff

P.C. HARRINGTON-JOHNSON EDITOR • A.H. PILL PRODUCER

A. VIDOW • T. RODGER • D. MUMFORD • W. STOBBS.

Our First Candle

Who would have thought a year ago,
At this same time of ice and snow,
That we should still be here to see,
M.M.C.'s first Anniversary.

When first keen followers used to meet,
Couched, cold upon a wooden seat,
The 'Reccy' Hut was uninviting,
But the subject was most exciting.

Then happy days we talked and planned,
Met by the pool amidst the sand.
Summer and Autumn passed apace.
Then indoors again — the cold washplace.

And now a year has gone and we
Remain, although impatiently,
Thinking of home and where we'll be,
For next year's Anniversary.

P. J. Benrose

165

The FLYWHEEL

'45'

NEW YEAR NUMBER

"KEEPS THE WORKS GOING ROUND ON THE IDLE STROKES"

Nº9 • JANUARY 1945 • STALAG IVB GERMANY •

Do the clouds seem to be breaking as we go to press with this copy— produced under what hardship? Cold, overcrowding, leaky roofs and the discouragements of low rations, "one-a-month- among-eight," and the bitterest frosts for years have conspired to delay the Supplement and we've had to suspend meetings. But "The Flywheel" keeps spinning on....

If there's one thing dead- certain-sure, it is that racing will enjoy a tremendous boom in the To-Be. Never have so many been taught to motorcycle, to find the fun of riding a lively and easily controlled two-wheel -er; never has a world been so shaken out of itself— and rarely has so much money been made available to so many,

All this means that there is going to be a general rush to let off steam, to escape the quiet monotony of Peace and Civvy Street — and the cheapest way is on a motor cycle. Young blood will have its fling!

Just think then, how we can reorganise, gear up our racing to the new drive. A machine built to the ideas described in the article inside, would sell better all over the world. It would not only give the proper emphasis on engine performance with reliability, that all racing brings, but would also place a long-needed spotlight on efficient, reliable, sturdier lighting sets – built lighter so they do not – for one thing – affect the steering

as do today's designs — and on far better and *efficient* silencing, and on comfort. Bits coming loose, wires chafing through, excessive noise — all damage the popularity of the game and tend to discourage good men from motorcycling, and that hits not only our club sport, but the trade, too...

There's a good time coming. Let us plan *well* to make the best of our liberty.

Editor

Hold fire on social! All is ready for our annual social and brew — entertainment, brew 'kit', etc., All we want is accommodation.

Riding through a town at 9.10 p.m. one evening in January 1939, at the height of a snowstorm I was troubled with my goggles constantly misting to such an extent that visibility was almost 'nil'. Without goggles I was almost blinded by the driving snow and had to proceed very warily until clear of the suburbs and street lamps. When I again tried my goggles I found to my astonishment, that they were perfectly clear and remained so for the rest of the run.

I had not at any time worn the goggles on my forehead, so they could not have been affected by body heat, and I am still at a loss to understand why after leaving the 'city lights' I was not further troubled. Can anyone enlighten me?

Prisoners of war returning home can, I understand, claim a petrol allowance to the tune of 300 miles per year of foreign service, the only stipulation being that the vehicle must be registered in the applicant's name. Circulation Chief Vidow assures me that he has no 'Blighty' Road Maps and so cannot very well assist 'Middle Easterners' in planning that two week's tour. Sorry, and all that.

Well, what did you think of the 'Beaumont'? For this preview of post-war models we must thank Bill May and congratulate him on being the possessor of a very retentive memory. His description makes some of the confirmed 'Triumph Twinites' not quite so confirmed.

Winds

ylch-y-Groes is a name that is often mentioned in club circles and in motoring articles, but relatively few people know what or where it is. From Welshpool, near the North Wales border, one should make for Dinas Mawdwyn which lies to the west, and taking the Bala road from there, drive as far as the Garage.

near the forked road and fill up. Leaving the main Bala road one should drive past the sign "Old Road to Bala Lake. Not recommended for Motorists", and drive for twenty minutes or so along one of the most delightful lanes I know, until a gate is reached (this should always be kept closed) and the famous hill is before you. Twenty yards from the gate is a right hand hairpin bend with a gradient of 1 in 4 followed by a fairly stiff 1¼ miles with an average gradient of 1 in 7. If the wind is down the valley it will greatly retard the rate of advance, and if it is blowing in the opposite direction it is guaranteed that the coolant in the 'rad' will be up to brewing temperature (212°F) in less than the time taken by the camp's best 'blower.'

Sports Cars
by
P. C. HARRINGTON-JOHNSON

BSA Scout

Those who know and like the Scout — and they are rightly many — look back with affection to the three-wheeler which fathered it, surely the sturdiest and friendliest little car Britain has ever produced. Somewhere about 1932 or '33 B.S.A. turned out a four wheel chassis with the 'nose' and body of the old 'trike' and a cranked trailing axle. The fabric body weighed 130 lbs. and the 1,021 c.c. air cooled 90° twin motor, o.h.v. is the finest and smoothest type of cyclecar motor. This engine had fixed cylinder heads and a huge bore cylinder — originally designed for a 9 h.p. cyclecar B.S.A. made in 1921. Its one fault was mechanical noise and a predisposition to run red hot. The cork insert clutch ran in oil and a 3-speed and reverse gearbox drove a bronze worm differential of exceptionally high workmanship. One internal-expanding brake was mounted on the differential, inside the boxnose channel-steel chassis. It worked indifferently well and was generally coated thickly with diff. oil — hence an incredible smell on long hills.... Two open half-shafts took the drive through fabric universals out to the hubs. The front wheels were very well and cleverly sprung on a "box" of quarter-elliptic leaf springs — almost unbreakable. The steering was peculiar and interesting — roughly described, a drum, intern-

ally toothed, driven by a cog, giving a reduction of 1½ turns of the wheel from lock to lock — with which an experienced driver can very nearly 'sidestep' his car. (Due to his brakes, he often *had* to.)

This twin job would do about 60 -'65 m.p.h, 40 -45 m.p.g. and had very good acceleration and superb pulling power. Speed increased to 70-

75 and acceleration also rose, if one carburettor was fitted to each of the low (4½ to 1) compression cylinders, without large increase in fuel consumption.

— "a most likeable, eyeworthy and zippy sporting car"...

About 1935 B.S.A. made a 1,072 c.c. sidevalve 4-cyl. tricar, with a two bearing 1½" diam. crankshaft. The gearchange, as hitherto, was a 'walking stick" on a ball and socket remote control, between the clutch and brake pedals. From this was produced the first Scout, in 1935 or '36. Using a trailing rear axle and the tricar power unit and nose, the Scout 9 was fitted with a very smart 360 lb metal-on-plywood two seater body of 'International type', bolt on wire wheels, a big tail tank and flowing mud-guards. The car handled superbly but would only do about 60 to 65 m.p.h. and, having no fan, used as much water as petrol. It was all but a dismal flop, for if driven hard the inadequately oiled big ends invariably 'ran'! Pneumatic upholstery was fitted and a bench type front seat (to the two seater).

Next year a bored-out and scaled-up Scout 10 came out with a 1,203 c.c. sidevalve motor and the gear change mounted on the wood dash in a 'brolly-handle' giving a flick-change. The chassis was still crab-track — front

wider than the back — but performance rose to a sturdy 70-74 and economy was about 35-40 m.p.g. The big engine gave a good top gear performance and some minor rally and hillclimb successes rewarded the wonderful handling and sturdy chassis. A four seater open and two seater coupé body came out and a two bladed fan, mounted on a bracket to the gear-box top, was driven by a speedo-cable in a bent iron pipe off the end of the generator.

In 1937 or 8 appeared the Series V Scout, with Bendix brakes on each front wheel, and in 1938-9 the Series VI dropped the crab-track, fitted Luvax 'shockers' in place of the old friction type, a gear (or chain?) drive, in a cast case, to fan off the fore end of the gear layshaft and a hub-width body, so that the 'two-seater' would easily take three in the bench front seat. A tremendous step forward was a three bearing crankshaft which put up top speed to a thoroughly dependable figure with adequate lubrication.

So, with the Series VI, the Scout remains — at about £170 — a most likeable, eyeworthy and zippy sporting car, whose delightful handling and sturdy build make it very tempting to Dominion users in particular and the sporting man in general.

Morgan 4 4

Sports Cars CONTD.

About the same time that the 'piled arms' produced their extremely likeable four cyl., the thirty year old Morgan concern brought out its Model F — a Ford 8 h.p. engine in a Z-shape channel steel chassis with the famous 'gas pipe'-and-

spring-king-post front axle introduced first in 1907 — and successfully used ever since. It was a natural but long awaited step to add another wheel. Around 1936 or 7 the dreams of 'Moggy' fans the world over were answered with the "Four-Four," a stumpy, handy 9 h.p. sports car.

Early models used the Coventry 'Climax' 1122c.c. o.h.v, 4-cyl. motor (to which one two or three carburettors can be fitted) and a possibly unique arrangement of a short cardan shaft from the clutch to a four

telescopic oil dampers.

The bodies, (two seater, four seater, and two seater drophead coupé), merit special attention, for H.S.F. Morgan has contrived the masterpiece of a ridiculously simple body, grotesquely ugly, that is yet

The 4/4 in Le Mans form

speed sports gearbox in the centre of the Z-shaped steel girder chassis, with a second short shaft to the back axle. Girling brakes were used, with pressed steel bolt-on wheels and the famous Morgan independant suspension and Newton type

most attractive and satisfyingly comfortable and 'cobby' – an amazing feat. The two seater is the only standard British car to fit a sorbo-padded leather arm-pad to the door tops. Petrol tanks are in the flat sided, "scullery steps" tail which also houses the twin spare wheels on two seaters.

Made exceedingly light — cars weigh complete between 10 and 12 cwts. only — the Four-Four has an astonishing performance, is very lively to drive, with a real racing 'feel' to the road-holding and handling, and hits 70 m.p.h. with the 1122 "C/C" motor, at 35 to 40 m.p.g.

In 1939 Morgans began to fit Standard '10', 4-cyl. sidevalve engines, with a leap in performance to an honest 80 m.p.h. and 45 m.p.g.. It is understood that odd cars have been privately fitted with Meadows o.h.c. 1496 c.c, 4-cyl. motors, of the Frazer-Nash type (which *just* fits in the chassis) and with Ford V8 22 h.p. units,

giving incredible zip and a comfortable 3-figure cruising speed! The "C/C" motor is alleged not to be quite up to the car's general standard of capabilities. (This defect is also levelled vigorously at the B.S.A. Scout by its devotees, who look for a less lazy motor with better performance.)

During its early life the Four-Four was copiously entered in big British trials and rallies, where its liveliness and handiness and smart lines earned it a widely envied reputation for a long list of shining successes. In 1938, too, a car was privately entered at the French Grand Prix d' Endurance 24 Heures at Le Mans in the 1100 class. Experience gained in this venture was embodied in

the special Le Mans model produced just before this war, with
a stripped body, strapped bonnet, cycle type wings and a
Burgess silencer draped along
the port side of the body most
rakishly. The motor, bored to
1100 c.c. for class racing, gave a
guaranteed top speed of 85 to 90.

Noteworthy features of the
cars are the floorboards,
fitting into the channels of the
chassis like German bedboards

and giving a sledge effect to
the car's underside; and the
cunning wood-frame sliding-
panel safety glass windows of
the coupé, which mount by bolts
to the door tops and give a
singularly snug closed, or completely open body.

The Four-Four costs
about £199. 10s. and is
probably the cheapest and
smallest pukka sports car of
raceable type on the market.

Economy Personified

by Geordie Elliot

It may surprise some
people how cheaply a
motor cycle can be run, provided the necessary determin-
ation is 'on tap'. The chappie

who has plenty of money and in-
tends to buy a new machine
needn't read this article; it is
intended for the man who has a
lot to do with his money and

can only afford a limited amount for the machine to which his heart yearns.

Tiger '100's' and other machines of similar type are very nice but the old saying, "Half a loaf is better than none," still goes. I was in that unlucky position in October '38 having just been married, not possessing a motor cycle and earning £2. 8s. a week, as a post-man — which everyone will agree is hardly a fortune. My personal pocket money from this was 3s. 0d. and 10s. 0d. per week overtime, out of which I used to pay for any cinemas, dances, etc., the two of us might attend.

I had at this time £5 which we had saved after our wedding expenses had been paid so I was looking for something very cheap and which had two wheels and an engine. I finally acquired, on a Wednesday morning, a 1929 B.S.A. 500 c.c. 'sloper,' for the 'magnificent' sum of £1. 17s. 0d.. After 'turning over' in one short burst, to show me that it would go, it refused to start, so I had to wheel it home, (an embarrassing ordeal for me.)

Between Wednesday and Friday night I stripped, cleaned and reassembled it, buy-ing only a secondhand magneto — which cost me 5s. 0d.. This mag-neto I had to fit with a $3/16$th steel plate to lift its spindle to the cor-rect height for the timing gear; it was a different make to the one originally on the machine. I kick-ed it over on Friday night and went for a short run.. Everything worked satisfactorily. It wasn't fast — maximum speed being about 65 m.p.h.—but I found that it would cruise quite comfortably at 55. During the time I had worked on the bike I had taxed and insured it, the Insurance being £2. 5s. (third party) for a year and the tax just under £1 (per quarter). A 'clever mathematician' working this out will see that the total cost to date with the machine now ready for the road, was £5. 7s. 0d, only 7s. 0d. having to be provided out of my 'pocket money'!

My wife and I travelled over 200 miles that first weekend with no trouble whatever and I found that petrol consumption was between 65 and 70 m.p.g.. Oil consumption was negligible, my usual practice being to put a pint in whenever I was a bit 'flush'. I ran this machine till I went 'on Draft' in April, 1940 and it gave sterling service, having absolutely nothing bought for it, except petrol and oil, in that time. My wife and I had a fortnight's holiday touring southern Scotland on it, and were often weekending with various relations. After the outbreak of war I ran it 73 miles *every* day (being stationed 36½ miles from home and spending every night there). I often got a 'headache' trying to figure out if I could afford a certain jaunt or not, but the fun we got out of that old machine was worth it ten times over. Fellows don't usually have to stretch things quite so fine as I had to then, fortunately, but I think it does show how little spare cash it can be done for.

STREAMLINE or Stagnate

BY 'KIWI' CURTIS

If all cars are to be dearer after the war, as seems probable, it is likely that the post-war sports job will be beyond the reach of the average person unless steps are taken to reduce the price margin that used to exist between the mass production and sports types.

No doubt sports car makers will not sit quietly back and see their products collecting dust in showrooms for lack of buyers with sufficient of the 'good stuff.' They will adopt various stratagems in order to offer the public something with a spot more pep than the average yet still not prohibitively higher in price.

The less pretentious efforts will probably be slightly hotted up versions of cheap, mass production chassis and they will not have much appeal to the enthusiast. At the other end of the scale Aston-Martin, Alta, Frazer-Nash, Bentley, Lagonda, etc., will still find a select, though possibly reduced market for cars of around £500 and more. It will be interesting to see what will develop in the £200 to £500 range.

Economy will have to be the big feature of such a class. The cars will need to be cheap to run and cost, preferably, not much over £300 to £400 in two or two-four seater form. This will mean a small capacity motor of 1100 c.c. to 1500 c.c. and as it will not be possible to turn out a really hot job within the price limit, some means will have to be adopted for getting the m.p.h. above average without much extra b.h.p.

Streamlining is the obvious answer — not streamlining as the Americans interpret it in terms of ornate chunks of bent tin, but scientific streamlining conforming to aircraft standards. It is an aspect of car design that received far too little attention before the war, especially by sports car designers whose ideals seemed to have changed little since the days of the old Bentleys and their ilk. However, there're signs on the continent that makers were doing something to reduce wind resistance, notably Adler and B.M.W. and one or two French sports cars entered in some of the European events just before the war.

Most interesting of all, but not designed as a sports car, was the 1100 c.c. Fiat with a special saloon body representing a definite attempt to get an aerodynamic form, albeit still deferring to some extent to conventional style. This car, tested at Brooklands by the "Motor" staff, returned some phenomenal figures. If memory does not err, the special-bodied chassis reached 90 m.p.h. compared with 70 m.p.h for the same chassis with standard body while petrol consumption was

W.5

about 45 m.p.g. against 30-35 m.p.g. in standard form. Coasting tests were made from various speeds to a standstill against a Morris 8 saloon. From 30 m.p.h. the Morris ran further but from all speeds above 30 the Fiat showed an increasing advantage till from 60 m.p.h. it ran over double the distance of the Morris. It also lapped Brooklands steadily at 80 m.p.h., averaging 30 m.p.g.. The only change made in the chassis was to raise the back axle ratio. The motor gave no more power than the ordinary 1,100 c.c. Fiat

so that all the advantages gained were due to the body and the careful undershielding.

These tests showed how much of the power of any car engine is absorbed by wind resistance. They also proved that efficient streamlining pays at low speeds – whereas it used to be considered a waste of time to bother about it at speeds below 100 m.p.h.. The Fiat showed it paid dividends from 30 m.p.h. up – handsome dividends at the speeds sports car drivers like to drive at. CONTINUED P.31

DECLINE OF A FORMULA

M. J. Airey

In many ways racing under the International Grand Prix formula in force at the outbreak of the present war had reached a climax. This unusual formula, it will be remembered, permitted a maximum engine size of 4½ litres without, and 3 litres with, compressor, as well as a maximum weight of 750 kilograms

of German successes, it attracted widespread interest not only from the motor racing public but also from a truly surprising number of manufacturers — no less than four from France announcing their intention of competing.

It was hoped in England that the 'Formula' E.R.A. would be ready in time.

W. S.

without fuel, oil, water and tyres. First introduced in 1938 after a long run

Both Alfa-Romeo and Maserati had high hopes of defeating the Mercédès and Auto-Union challenges although it was rumoured that 'Il maestro' - Tazio Nuvolari was to handle a German Machine.

Of the French cars, Delahaye and Delage

tradition. "Phi-Phi" Etancelin had been asked to handle one of the new Talbot-Darracqs whose engines would be made in both permissable sizes.

both favoured the larger engine size using a V 12-cylinder formation. The former marque was to be run by L'ecurie Bleu under Madame Schell with René Dreyfus as team leader, whilst J. Paul was commissioned to drive the latter. Ettore Bugatti was said to be producing a straight eight supercharged 3 litre model which would depart from Molsheim

The Mercédès drivers remained unchanged whilst Auto-Union had naturally to replace Rosemeyer. Both firms were concentrating on 3 litre units.

With such a fine array of the world's best cars and drivers in combat, interest ran high in anticipation of the coming season. When René Dreyfus enjoyed initial and, indeed, unexpected

success against the complete Mercédès team enthusiasm increased and 'wise' heads began to predict a supremacy of the un-supercharged type. Further to support their opinion, the Delahaye repeated its successes in the Cork Grand Prix although there its strongest opposition came from its French rival – the new streamlined 'monoplace' Bugatti driven by Jean Pierre Wimille and from "B. Bira" in his four-year-old ex-Whitney Straight Maserati. The Bugatti acquitted itself admirably, proving fastest over the timed ¼ mile at 145 m.p.h.

However—as soon as Mercédès had their cars 'au point' and Auto-Union were ready, the blown 3 litre engine monopolised the formula.

There followed a succession of German wins of which the two most noteworthy were the late Dick Seaman's success in the German Grand Prix and Nuvolari's Auto-Union Donington victory.

Of the rest of the field, the straight eight Maseratis were outclassed and in a vain attempt to catch the German cars, Alfa Romeo tried 8, 12 and even 16 cylinders! In its 'dummy run' in the International Trophy Race at Brooklands the 4½ litre Delage caught fire, crashed and tragically killed a number of spectators including T. Murray Jamieson. Our own E.R.A. unfortunately failed to materialise while the Darracqs proved too slow.

It was evident in the following year that

Auto Union and Mercedes Benz with their experienced drivers — they had Caracciola, Nuvolari and Seaman, remember — would

least gave the German team something to think about.

mall wonder perhaps that with the arrival of

repeat their 1938 successes unless unless any of their rivals found extraordinary speed. Even if the formula was not considered as played out, its only remaining interest was the brilliant exhibition Luigi Villoresi whose dashing driving of an improved 3 litre Maserati at

the new 1½ litre E.R.A. to challenge the new four cylinder Maserati and small Alfa Romeo, attention was being focussed upon "voiturette" racing — but that's another story.

"Pardon!! My mistake"

by Tom Swallow

Fred sat in a seat at the rear of the darkened cinema, blissfully unaware of what was being enacted upon the screen, when all at once he came back to earth with a bump. Was that rain he could hear? Yes, it most certainly was. "My dear," he whispered, "I must slip out and raise the hood on the car or it will be swamped. Wont be a minute"

Feeling his way out he was painfully aware of the size of his feet as he blundered against several pairs of legs, and was rewarded for his pains by a number of quiet curses. On reaching the aisle he hurried to the door and ran across the road, in the pouring rain, to the car park, across the way.

Hell, he thought, where did I leave the car, oh yes, I remember, up at the corner. Not there! That fool of an attendant must have moved it. Pretty hopeless to look for it in this dark. Ah! Here we are. He didn't shift it very far. Wish I had splashed the extra few quid and bought a saloon, but the tourer looked very nice in the Morris agents and that grey finish does look nice when the sun's shining. Wont be long now. Drat the rain, will it never cease! I *would* leave my coat back there with Mary. Come on, my beauty, let's have you up. Ah! that's better. Hood up and side shields fixed. S'funny, though, I thought I'd left them at home. Must be mistaken!

The little Morris '8' was soon ship-shape and Fred was about to return to his waiting fiancé when to his horror he noticed that one of the rear tyres was flat.

What should he do? Mend it now or leave it till after? He really was enjoying himself before this rain. But no; he must not be selfish. He would prove to his Mary that he thought

enough of her to get wet for her sake.

With a shrug he turned to the toolbox and had a job to find his tools. His torch was missing but in spite of this he struggled manfully, overcoming all sorts of difficulties and getting drenched to the skin. His good temper slowly left him until by the time he had lost the skin off his knuckles, he was soon in a livid temper, which was not improved when he sat in a puddle.

At last he was finished and staggered into the little car and felt for the spare packet of cigarettes that were always there, but even they were missing. "What the hell's the matter with this car?" he muttered.

The "Odeon" disgorged its crowd and soon he saw Mary stepping daintily around the puddles and heading towards him. "Coo-ee", he cried "over here". Mary clambered into the seat and glowered. "Have you brought my mac," he asked. "Have I Hell," she responded, "What do you think I am? A pack horse?" Fred collapsed like a pricked balloon. He slunk back into the theatre and returned in a wicked frame of mind to find a little crowd around his car and an argument in full swing. Someone was trying to get Mary out of her seat.

Dashing up, he cried "What's going on here?" "This is my car," said a stranger. "Like Hell it is", replied our hero, "I bought this six weeks ago".

"**N**ot on your life," came the answer. "You will please observe the number is ALL 40. My car. Perhaps that

similar model yonder, UPU 2, is yours."

Fred's jaw dropped, for the moon, which suddenly

peeped through the clouds revealed a similar model, his car, standing, minus its hood, in a big puddle; and there was no 'flat'.

Mary refused to budge, so the stranger offered to drive her home. She, without so much as a glance at the beaten Fred, accepted, and as our friend was sitting in a puddle trying to start *his* car, the stranger's voice came

CONTINUED ON P. 31

The "EXETER"

OBSERVED
SECTION
BEGINS

by TOM . SWALLOW

The first important event in the sporting motorist's calendar is The London- Exeter Trial. Organised by the Motor Cycling Club of Great Britain (M.C.C.), this event attracts some 6 or 7 hundred entrants from the car and motor cycle world, and if you are watching the event you can expect to see all types of vehicles from 125 c.c. two-strokes to 3-litre Bentleys.

To take part in the event one must be a member of the M.C.C. and pay the entrance fee of £1. Three widely separated points are selected for the start — Stratford-upon-Avon, Virginia Water and Exeter and competitors may start from any of these points, (after notifying the 'powers that be', of course) and proceed by his own route to the first check (a road-house on the Bristol — Bridgewater road) thence, via Taunton, to Exeter — where No 1 is due in at 0430 a.m. for breakfast and even at this early hour the waitresses at Deller's Cafe are nipping around. After a nice refreshing wash one sits down to a beautiful breakfast of... (censored). Ninety minutes is the time allowed for breakfast 'break' and at 6 a.m. No 1 climbs back into the saddle and rides away with headlamps blazing, in the cold morning.

Soon the main roads are left behind as the route takes us towards the first 'section' and the rider or driver must keep his wits about him if he is to keep out of the ditches that line the

torchlights of a fair crowd of spectators can be seen amongst the trees. The hill itself is steep, rock-strewn and slippery, and contains one or two hairpin bends, and it is woe betide any man whose

twisting, turning, climbing lanes and byeways.

Suddenly one leaves the road altogether, crosses a stream and head between trees up a steep slimy hill to the first observed section, Fingle Ridge, It is still dark and perhaps raining or snowing but even so, the

lights have failed before this. (I know!)

From here the trial must be taken seriously. 'Stop and Start', 'Braking' and 'Acceleration Tests' are the order of the day, and simple though they may be, after twelve, or so, hours in the saddle even the simplest test requires concentration. In 1939 Simm's Hill was introduced as a Bonus Hill and a clean climb of this hill would wipe out a failure in any other one section. There was a 'way round' for anyone who did not wish to attempt the hill, which proved to be com-paratively easy, although very steep and containing a 'sharpish' right hand bend. This 'terror' was 'tamed' by a real good sur-face but many entrants failed through wheelspin.

At 14.30 hours No. 1 is somewhere near the finishing point — 'The Grand', Bournemouth, about 16½ hours after leaving Strat-ford, so that, after booking in, a competitor can either turn round and 'go home' or get in a few hours sleep before spending the Saturday evening as it should be spent, returning home on the morrow.

Awards are of the 'Gold', 'Silver', or 'Bronze' variety and no-one can win the trial out-right. Every finisher is, therefore, almost assured of an award of some sort, and it is because of the high number of finishers that the entry fee is so high.

The speeds demanded are not high and any type of vehicle (commercial vehicles are barred) will assure an enthus-iastic owner of an exciting week, a good time, and perhaps, a medal for the collection.

It is to be hoped that the M.M.C. badge will be well in evidence at the next 'Exeter.'

'TT' Stands for Tourist Trophy

by P.C. HARRINGTON-JOHNSON

Should we keep the T.T.? This question was being asked in 1939 in the British motor press and some interesting information was given. While, considering the 1939 T.T. results — one British win and two seconds in three classes from keen foreign competion — one cannot avoid a certain suspicion of "sour grapes", there is little doubt that for some years — since the early '30's, in fact — the I.o.M. racing has kept up its *spectacular* value at the *steady loss* of its *usefulness* to the ordinary rider.

The Italians, for one, have found a very attractive and practical solution to the difficult position — a Grand Prix Touring racing class. You can, of course, order that sort of thing to be done — and it *is* done — in a fascist country.

Consider the '39 I.o.M. machine — Norton single, 'Velo' twin, B.M.W. twin, A.J.S. four — and think how far they differ from the stock replica on sale to the public. How would it be to use such a machine on the road — terrific speed, acceleration, perfect steering and brakes, but what about noise, lights, cleanliness? The racing trend is for a blown multi — yet how many blown o.h.c. multis are seen on the road?

Granted that racing is the research field of the trade, how many makers *do* race — four, in all Britain! The others just don't bother — and save the dough. They say, some of them, that they are not interested in racing as it is done today — it's too expensive and cliquey.

bring in something like the Italian Touring Grand Prix." It was realised that the Senior T.T. has a draw as a spectacle exceeding anything else on the calendar and brings enormous tourist crowds and money to the Isle of Man. Let us keep the Senior unaltered, therefore, but let's bring in a more useful type

MOTO GUZZI

So the motor press in England, summarising the matter, suggested "Keep the T.T. — but drop, say, the "350" and perhaps the lightweight, and

of event that will definitely benefit not only the trade but the riding public, too.

The way Musso did it was, through his

chief of motor sport, to devise a new type of race and insist on all big makers building and entering machines for it. The Grand Prix Touring Race Class — several were held in 1938-40 — was for a stock model of 500c.c., which had to use pump fuel sold to the public, and *had* to be ridden *in full road trim, silencer, lamp, battery and hooter.* And all these had to work, *before* and *after* the race

Naturally, machines were of 'Replica' pattern, but Guzzi and Benelli (of the half-dozen big Italian makes competing) both produced spring frame 'Tourers', capable of a fully equipped 110-115 m.p.h. on 50/50! Beside their interest, the races attracted great attention and were a big success.

Think what this sort of bike would be like to ride — reliable high speed all over (and they had spring frames and racing brakes, too!) — and how it would sell in the export market. How many riders could buy one and use it, compared with those who can buy and use the slower and less well-equipped replicas sold so far?....

And if it proved difficult to get firms to support the class, why not issue W.D. and Govt. contracts only to those firms toeing the line? It's been done — successfully, on the continent, before....

CONTINUED FROM P. 17

It should be comparatively simple for a sports car builder to design a two-seater body which will permit an 1100 c.c. chassis at least to equal the Fiat figures and as the motor need not be particularly hot the first cost could be kept within reach of the average enthusiast. I, for one, would look with considerable favour on something having the general appearance of a pub from the litter of a Grand Prix Merc with better than 90 m.p.h. maximum, acceleration in keeping and 30 m.p.g. at 80 m.p.h.

CONTINUED FROM P. 24

over to him "Awfully nice of you to change my wheel, old chap, cheerio!"

 he last the unhappy man saw of his downfall was its rear number plate as it turned into the main road. ALL FOUR NOUGHT.

COMPARISON

Next month we propose to feature, pictorially, a post-war sports saloon, manufactured the famous Aston-Martin, the 'Atom'. The main interest to us is the immediate similarity to our own brain child, the 'Ideal Car.' Constructional and performance details of the 'Atom' are entirely unknown — but, there is room for much speculation and still more comparisons.

Do you know?

That Rudge Whitworth Motor Cycles, Ltd., has discontinued manufacture; only cycles and auto-cycles are now being produced? All spares and servicing has been taken over by Godfrey's Ltd.

That the Armstrong-Saurer Deisel engine rights were purchased by the Nuffield Group — Morris Commercials blossoming out post-war?

That a petrol allowance for 300 miles travelling, per year of foreign service, is available on return to 'Blighty'? It is necessary that the applicant

has to have a motor vehicle fully registered, taxed and insured in his own name before claim is made.

That the price of petrol per gallon is 2s.0½d? (September '44). Not bad after five years of war!

That more than 100,000 motor tractors have been manufactured for agricultural use during the war by England?

That South Africa has a potential market for 150,000 cars? The yearly consumption is slightly more that 30,000 and they are ready to import 15,000, within six months of the conclusion of hostilities, from America. Has our industry turned its eyes this way?

'That the possibility of any future world shortage of rubber has been

eliminated by the recent process of artificial rubber production. This new method was developed by two South Africans — who claim to produce synthetic rubber at 1s. 10d per ton instead of the previous best price which was 14/ per ton.

Hints & Tips

A useful dodge for car or bike for wet weather running is to cut an ordinary tennis ball in half and fit one half over each plug, running the high tension lead through a small hole. This will keep rain and splashes off, and prevent wet coat tails from shorting the plug.

Any bike can be made much more comfortable to ride by cutting a piece of up-to-½" sponge rubber mat to fit between the saddle cover and the spring top. It may bulge the cover a bit, but will soon shape to the rider.

CLUB NEWS

After twelve months of active 'club life' the 'raison d' etre' seems to be missing in the life of many club members since we were forced to suspend the club meetings and the temptation to 'hit the hay' has grown stronger. Our Aussi members were the first to hibernate and it is only to renew the store of 'nuts' (P. Ps. in Kriegsgefangenenspruch) that they venture past the doors of their hut. ● ●

We may be down, but we're not out, as the appearance of this mag. proves, and it is hoped that an improvement in weather and accommodation will soon allow us to renew our 'gathering of the clans.'

But while you are lying in the 'Flea pit' you have plenty of time to think so we expect to be inundated with suggestions and articles in the near future. ● ●

Those of you who find a 'minus' temperature to keep two feet 'on the deck' will, I'm sure, join me in raising the proverbial hat to our energetic production staff who labour hour after hour at their unremunerative task, in spite of the intense cold. ● ●

What was the most interesting lecture, debate or topic of the past year? I think we must give full marks to the 'Ideal Car,' our brain-child which was rejected, wrongly, it seems, by the

Campo P.G. 70 Auto Club, of summer skies. The Quizes proved to be very popular as did member's experiences, of which I think 'Geordie' Elliot's 'School for D.Rs.' was the most amusing but I think the informal nights, such as 'Unusual Experiences', 'Making Do', etc., take a bit of beating for sheer enjoyment

Flash!! latest prices from home

Another service by Swallow! The following prices received by Dec. 8th '44 letter from Tommy, Senior.

ARIEL.. 1938 350 Red Hunter, one owner. £50. 600 s.v, Aug. '37, 7,000 miles. nearest offer to.. £65.

A recent letter in the camp speaks of a recently purchased brand new 1944 model 350 Ariel, which, whilst not a startling fact in itself, would seem to indicate that we shall not have to wait long for 'pukka' civvy models, as they have, in fact, been in production, on a reduced scale, the whole time.

DOUGLAS.. 1936 600 c.c. Aero Sports, Launch sports sidecar, perfect condition. £47. 10s.

RUDGE.. '39 Rapid 250 o.h.v. actual mileage 893. Nearest to £60. Ulster, May '38, 499 c.c. 6-day trial model, very fast, 78 Gns.

More prices next month.

CONTENTS

The FLYWHEEL

KEEPS THE WORKS GOING ROUND ON THE IDLE STROKES

NO. 10 • MARCH 1945 • MUHLBERG ON ELBE

There is a tide in the affairs of men which, taken at the flood, leads on. . . .

We're looking forward now, most of us. Not only the outside influences are making for a hopeful future. It's in the time of year. Spring is coming, with its yearly promise of the roads once more. Easter is just round the next bend, with its busy programme of racing, trials and a long weekend's touring.

So this issue we mix both hopes — the sportsman's, for his meeting (first of the summer's fixture list) and the tourist-family man — who has laid his machine up for the winter and is about to burst forth with his second quarter's licence — and perhaps, in a deeper significance, for those of us whose "wheels" have been blocked up now these many weary years, waiting... There'll be much to do.

Editor.

Reawakening :—

Your reign has ended, now 'tis time to sleep,
Awaiting for the greens to turn to gold,
No more the Ice-trapped boughs will weep,
For robins garnering in the cold.

Gentle snow gives place to March's gusts,
While teeming rivers swell to overflow,
A crocus head through dripping emerald thrusts,
Beside a blank where mosses grow.

Each creature wakes from hibernation,
To greet returning heralds of the Spring,
The world awaits in expectation
For better times will soon begin.

P. J. Bemrose

With five inch tyres, sprung seat pillar and spring frame the 'Beaumont' promises to be the most comfy thing on two wheels and should attract many would-be motorists, who, according to Sir Miles Thomas, vice-chairman of Nuffields, will find that motoring is a little too expensive. The use of 'infinitely variable gears' makes the process of 'driving' even more simple and one wonders whether a self-starter will be fitted to the final models. Many of the 'pukka' enthusiasts may shudder at such a thought, but the kick-starter has frightened many a 'border-liner' from joining the ranks and except for the increase in cost there is no reason why it should not be fitted.

A number of old 'kriegies' had been chatting with some new Yanks and were amazed and terribly impressed by their casual remarks about 80, 90 and 100 h.p. cars. What they did not know was that the h.p. quoted was 'brake horse power' and that the h.p. usually associated with British cars is not h.p. at all but really a standard of measurement for taxation purposes. They were surprised to hear that the Wolseley

'18', by American rating would be a Wolseley '80', because it developes 80 b.h.p. and their impression of monster cars faded considerably. Good sales figures though, don't you think?

WINDS

It is interesting to note that we in England although we have (in 1940) only one mechanically propelled vehicle per 18 of population, as compared with America's 1 per 5 have almost twice as many vehicles per mile of road. The actual figures are 14.5 vehicles per mile in Britain and 8.2 in the 'States', and unless we have some big 'post-war' road schemes afoot we are likely to become even more crowded, as the number of cars in 'Blighty' is increasing steadily by some 6% per annum, whereas the roads are only increasing by 1½% over a corresponding period. This latter figure is not just during the war, but over a period of thirty years.

Forerunners in motor-cycle exports to U.S.A of interest was the 60 odd Ariel Square 4's purchased by the New York State Police. They were standard machines, but fitted with crash bars, sirens, etc..

Sports Cars - H.R.G. Maurice Airey

There exists, unquestionably, on the British market a demand, albeit limited, for a light car, which while possessing individuality, adheres to well-tried principles of design and gives something above average in the way of performance, finish and manufacture, without considerable first cost.

Introduced by H.R. Godfrey in 1937 to meet this demand, the 12 h.p. H.R.G. at £395 has a special appeal to the sportsman and competition driver. Eschewing all unnecessary fittings like synchromesh to which the present-day driver is accustomed, the specification includes a 69 × 100 m.m. 1.496 c.c. o.h.c. Meadows engine from which the drive is taken to the spiral bevel rear axle through a single dry plate clutch and a Moss 4 speed crash type gear box with remote control gate change. The fitting of a tubular front axle and quarter-elliptic springs may be traced to the G.N. for which the H.R.G's creator, in collaboration with Archie Frazer Nash, was responsible. Rudge wire wheels with knock-on caps are fitted while the brakes are mechanically operated in large-diameter drums.

tilising short swept wings, the 2-door open body is of International type which provides room for luggage behind the two bucket seats. From the where the radiator is set-well behind the axle, to the tail which takes

B.T.

the form of a large-capacity slab fuel tank situated under the spare wheel the car has a distinctive business-like appearance.

evoid of all frills the H.R.G. weighs remarkably little, which is partly responsible for its magnificent acceleration, making it eminently suitable for use in speed trials and road racing in which events, incidentaly, it has performed well.

n the competition world, particularly in trials and driven by P.C.T. Clarke, Robins and Green it quickly acquired respect. P.C.T. Clarke's Le Mans venture in 1938 proved an entire success and led to the marketing at £425 of a special Le Mans model with a highly tuned engine and streamlined tail housing an extra large fuel tank. While standard models were genuine everyday 80 m.p.h. cars, the Le Mans model which Clark has used on Brooklands Outer Circuit, tops 90.

For 1939 a smaller car appeared. The 10 h.p. o.h.c. Singer engine of 1074 c.c. was used in this model which perhaps is best described as a scaled down edition of the 1½ litre. Priced at £285, in every way it maintained the high reputation established by its bigger brother. A maximum of over 70 could be reached under everyday conditions while, although no acceleration figures are available here, the reader is assured that they are startlingly good.

The price of the larger car was increased to £424. 10s. when the 1497 c.c. o.h.c. Singer engine replaced the Meadows used hitherto. At the Le Mans in 1939 Peter Clark and Marcus Chambers continuing their good work added to British and H.R.G. prestige.

The manufacturer's phrase "Built by enthusiasts for enthusiasts" adequately sums up the H.R.G.

SELECTED
Prices for January '45

1939 Velocette 350c.c. M.A.C. Perfect Condition, 2 new covers, spare clutch, complete tools, Storm coat, waders, goggles, Everything for the road — £70.

95 gns.; ARIEL '4', May 1939, 600 c.c.; one owner. Bargain £47-10s.; COVENTRY EAGLE PULLMAN, 250 o.h.v. Blackburne, spring frame, dyno, pillion. All in new condition.

Preparation

by Tom Swallow

The opening of the Lenten season means, among other things, to the amateur Racing Motor Cyclist that he has some six weeks in which to have his machine ready for the starting line on Easter Monday, on which day the racing season is opened (perhaps in a blaze of sunshine, perhaps in a flurry of snow.) At this time there is usually a lot of work to be done and a peep into the workshop will give us an idea of the actual position.

For financial reasons the old model is going to be "flogged" for yet another season and the winter work entailed by such a decision is tremendous. However, much of this work has been started already and the work on the engine should, by now, be almost completed and all the new and 'renovated' parts be neatly packed away ready for the great day when re-assembly begins.

A new big-end bearing has, perhaps, been fitted and the flywheel assembly, (which "keeps the works going round on the idle strokes") has been lightened and polished. Any work on this part of the engine should always be attended to by the works, as it is very difficult for an amateur, with his limited equipment, correctly to line-up and balance, a pair of flywheels, and in any case it *may* be detrimental to the engine to lighten them. The maker would know.

A new high compression piston has been obtained and the ring gap 'adjusted' and the head, also, has come in for a lot of attention, new valves, guides and seat inserts having been fitted, as well as stronger valve springs.

B efore the engine is re-assembled the 'oil-drag' question is to be tackled seriously and an aluminium plate has to be fitted to cover up the reinforcing ribs inside the crankcase.

F ollowing the advice of the maker, Castrol 'R' is being dropped, and a normal light mineral oil used, thus making it essential that all oil pipes, ducts, reservoirs and pumps are absolutely free from 'R' before assembling.

T he carburettor is being left strictly alone and the machine sent to the Perry Barr factory for tuning when everything is ready, but the magneto has been back to Rugby and is resting on the kitchen shelf where it will be free from damp.

T he frame has been reset and cellulosed, but the new sprint tank has not yet been delivered. (An urgent letter must be sent off immediately). The brakes have yet to be relined — the rear drum could do with being 'skimmed'— the wheel bearings removed, cleaned, checked for wear, and replaced, and if the first meeting is Red Marley it will be necessary to use a pair of old 'combs' for spiking purposes. To do this, literally hundreds of holes have to be punched, bored, burned or bitten through these outer covers and the necessary bolts fitted. On a gradient of 1 in 1½, such tyres are very useful, particularly if it is raining and there is a few inches of mud at the bottom of the hill.

On top of this, the exhaust wants 'de-coking', clutch relined, mudguards fitting, saddle recover-ing, controls and cables checking and replacing where necessary and the gearbox still requires attention. Dozens of little odds and ends want seeing to.

Yes, there is still a lot of work to be done, letters to be written, phone calls to be made and I fear a lot of midnight oil must be burned if the model is to be ready for a try-out, (and it must be) a fortnight before the great event. But this is half the fun — trying to get a little more power from the old engine — and he who can afford a new machine each year misses much of the fun of preparation.

But what, you may ask, is the object

Continued P. 34

HIGHLAND
'Steed'

by Andrew Blair

About 1932 I decided to buy a small car, having up till then ridden motor cycles of the ultra small variety. So with a limited amount of cash available I set out in search of a cheap little car.

Eventually I discovered a likely-looking 7·17 h.p. horizontally opposed twin-cylinder Jowett with two-seater all-weather body, manufactured in either 1924-25 (I can't quite remember which). Some of the details I do remember.

The steering was epicyclic, of the direct or semi-direct type. The brakes were the old band type, the foot brake operating on a drum just behind the gear box, while the handbrake operated on the rear wheels only. The gearbox was of the old three-speed and reverse "crash" type, gate change; the clutch was of the cone type, using asbestos string strengthened with bronze wire, but really gave excellent service.

The steering, which I took an intense dislike to, I changed for a more modern type of similar make, which this time required two turns of the wheel for lock to lock instead of just under one. I almost forgot to mention that the carburettor fitted was the standard Zenith, which some master hand had tuned really well.

I drilled the induction manifold and fitted a suction-type windscreen wiper, the tube of which I used to disconnect at the windscreen after the engine warmed up, thus providing a type of variable mixture to the carburettor and as my normal runs were about fifty or sixty miles, petrol con-

So I felt very proud of my purchase.

The hill climbing ability was good; tested out with two up, and with what is easily the largest body fitted on a car of that h.p., on such hills as Rest-and-be-Thankful, (1 in 7), Whistlefield (1 in 6), Train-a-four (1 in 3) and the Devil's Elbow, Glenshee.

Alas, just after more than a summer's running

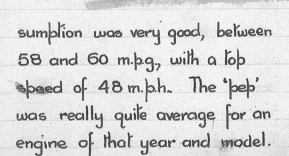

sumption was very good, between 58 and 60 m.p.g., with a top speed of 48 m.p.h. The 'pep' was really quite average for an engine of that year and model.

of really trouble-free motoring, I had the misfortune to skid and overturn, badly damaging the bodywork, but still leaving the

CONTINUED ON P.34

FORMULA REVIVAL

by Maurice Airey

It remains significant that at least five of the world's most celebrated motor manufacturers—namely, E.R.A, Mercédès-Benz, Alfa-Romeo, Alta and Maserati, had, in spite of the International Grand Prix formula operating in 1938/9, chosen to produce cars of 'voiturette' (1500 c.c.) size. That such importance was attached to the value of 1½ litre racing indicates that a revised formula, embracing this size of car, would receive strong International support, particularly since a decline in competitive spirit had reduced Grand Prix racing to a mere procession. In fact the adoption of a 1500 c.c. formula was regarded in some circles as a certainty, had not war intervened.

Of course, light car racing in the past has not been neglected. From the time when the original 1½ litre formula produced such fine cars as the straight eight Delage, 'immortal' Bugatti, and Talbot Darracq, voiturette racing has proved very popular. Motor racing crowds were treated to some of the keenest competition at the period between such exponents as Henry Seagrave, Louis Chiron, Malcolm Campbell and Keneton Lee Guiness — to mention only a few— and to the first British Grand Prix which was held at Brooklands in 1926 and which gave Talbot-Darracq a "1, 2" victory.

Quite naturally, as Grand Prix cars became larger and faster, light car racing received less attention until what may, perhaps, accurately be described as the M.G. era. In the early '30's the accepted limit of light car size - as far as racing was concerned - was 1,100 c.c. Within this category the M.G. Magnette excelled itself.

effect on Continental road circuits. It was not until the E.R.A. made its appearance, however, that actual 1½ litre racing resumed something of its former importance. At the commencement of the 1935 season began the unforgetable E.R.A. onslaught on European events. Handled not only by a team of 'works' drivers including Mays, Cook, Fairfield, Dobson and Howe, but also by private enthusiasts

— '39 1½ LITRE E.R.A —

Amongst others, Whitney Straight, H.G. Hamilton, and R.J.B. Seaman showed its paces to good

like Seaman and Bira, this make of car proved unbeatable by any of its contemporaries.

In passing, mention must be made of the 1926 Delage in which R.J.B. Seaman put up those well-remembered performances that won him recognition as an exponent comparable with the best.

Italy's answer to the E.R.A — the six cylinder Maserati — failed to check this onslaught even when handled by Luigi Villoresi and J. P. Wakefield.

During 1938, instead of being concentrated upon the G. P. formula, E.R.A. policy, dictated partly by financial considerations, was directed towards the production of a vastly improved 1½ litre machine. How great a threat this new vehicle was considered in Italy may be guaged from the appearance in 1938, not only of a modified Maserati, using four cylinders instead of six, but of an entirely new Alfa Romeo as well. This was not all. A challenge in the shape of a team of 1½ litre Mercédès materialised while Geoffrey Taylor had his creation, the Alfa V8, almost ready.

Curiously enough, although many of the cars mentioned have distinguished themselves individually, they have not yet properly come to grips. The new E.R.A., for instance, not only broke its class lap record in practise at Rheims but was leading the field at Berne when Dobson crashed. This latter event was won by Wakefield driving the new Maserati whilst the Swiss, A. Hug, was successful at Rheims in a similar car. The Mercédès

CONTINUED P.22

SHOULD THERE BE A "T.T"?

An Answer

BY BILL MAY

The above question asked by P.C. Harrington-Johnson, in the New Year number of "Flywheel," is so outspoken and contrary to my own opinions that I felt I should answer it immediately, and in giving my criticisms of this article, at the same time giving my reasons for the continuance of the T.T. as it was known pre-war.

Having read every edition of "The Motor Cycle" and "Motor Cycling" from 1934 until August 17th 1944 I am reasonably well acquainted with the average motorcyclist's opinion, as expressed in the correspondence columns. The title-subject of this article was the theme of an intensive controversy which raged intermittently for over two years, until early in 1944. Graham Walker asked none other than Joe Craig to write an article on the subject, and to give his opinion on "Does racing benefit the ordinary rider?" In his article Mr Craig answered both questions with a very emphatic "Yes" and in this article I will, in answering 'P.C.', be quoting the ex-Norton wizard, as the article he wrote proved that the opinions I held on the subject were identical to his own.

Every pre-war motor cyclist worthy of the name was, I thought, acquainted with the facts which accounted for our first complete, total defeat by the 'foreign menace' of recent years, in the 1939 Senior T.T., 'P.C.' evidently is not, so I will outline what I can recall of the circumstances. In 1938, after their usual victorious season, Norton Motors announced their intention of withdrawing from official racing for the next year, the reason now being obvious. The Norton machines ridden in the '39 Senior T.T. by Messrs Daniel, Frith and White, were privately entered and were in fact their 1938 machines.

Owing to the untimely demise of Mr. Harold Willis designer for Veloce Ltd., a few weeks before the T.T. the Velocette Twin could not be made ready for the actual race, so Stanley Woods competed also on his 1938 mount. Surely this cannot be thought by 'P.C.' to be the best opposition that Britain's industry could produce. If he was thinking of the A.J.S. 'four', then all I can say is that at best all that the most optimistic A.J.S. enthusiast could expect was a 'third', considering the calibre of the opposition, even though it be 1938 mounted. I might add in passing, that the record lap established by Harold Daniel in 1938, still stands to his credit today, at a speed of 91 m.p.h.

How many blown o.h.c. multis does 'P.C.' expect to see on the road when the two manufacturers using such machines for racing had not overcome their teething troubles? He admits that racing is the research

field of the industry, and yet asks why the machines are not on the road when obviously there has been no time for complete research. Admittedly only four manufacturers officially supported racing, but the others were only too prompt in following the racing makes in using any new development found advantageous in racing. The most noticable example of this being the prompt use of light alloy for barrel and head in their so called 'sports' machines, and for one instance in particular I have only to quote the B.S.A. 'Gold Star.' I personally cannot recall ever hearing of a B.S.A. machine officially entered in racing. My opinion of why other makers do not compete is that it is only too obvious that the opposition is too great. It would also be obviously foolish to drop the Junior or Lightweight because of the different problems which arise with the smaller sizes.

In 1939 Graham Walker organised at Donington a Clubman's meeting in which all machines had to be fully equipped, and at the completion of each event the failure of any item of equipment such as lighting sets spelt disqualification even although the competitor may have been first over the line. This method of developing accessories is surely better than having official entries from manufacturers with the attendant possibilities of special machines being used even in the face of the most stringent regulations. Whether a certain manufacturer was in favour or not, any one of his catalogued machines would possibly be used, which would ensure improvments found necessary to the equipment being fitted to all machines. I hardly think that any of our manufacturers would respond to being ordered by the government to produce a special machine for such an event, in fact I think that any such proposals would very easily start quite a sizeable revolution, except that is amongst such members of the community with Facist tendencies, but after the last six years I don't think there will be many with such inclinations.

So Guzzi and Benelli are able to produce fully equipped tourers capable of 115 m.p.h. when our Tiger '100' supersports twin (the Guzzi being a single) can only reach the magic century. Possibly the best machine for comparison with the Guzzi is our own International Norton. It is, I think, one of the best road machines of single cylinder replica type produced at home and yet it is only capable of approximately 95 m.p.h. Are we asked to believe that the Italians can obtain an extra 20 m.p.h. from a machine of basically identical construction?

Although spring frames have been on the market for, I believe, 25 years prior to 1939, it wasn't until they were found to be a necessary

beam. What price that the majority of the leading makes will be fitting telescopic front forks on their post-war machines? Who will deny then, that racing developed that item of equipment? The first time it was seen on a British machine was in the T.T.— fitted to Nortons who themselves

part of the machine for racing, that they were marketed and sold in any quantity by the leading makes, especially the non-racing ones such as Ariel, Levis, Montgomery, Panther and Sun-

were beaten to it by B. M. W. but at the same time first used by that marque for racing.

I think therefore, that we should keep the T.T. as it is for development of the machine, and for the marvelous spectacle it provides, but at the same time institute events of the type organised by Graham Walker, and let the clubmen prove to themselves and the manufacturers just what parts of the machine are weak. In this way I don't think the manufacturers would be long in improving any article of equipment found to be defective.

Might I, in conclusion, suggest that we have a discussion in the club on this subject, as I feel that although I have rambled on to a considerable length, there are several points on which I should like to lay more emphasis.

FORMULA REVIVAL CONTD FROM P. 16.

and Alfa Romeo had proved victorious at Tripoli and in the Coppa Acerbo respectively.

When these machines eventually come together the results should prove interesting.

Comparison-"Ideal Car-Aston Martin"Atom"

Once more we regret to postpone comparing our "Brain Child" with the 'Atom." However, the necessary material is now at hand and April's edition should see the outcome.

BEST for the BRITON

by 'KIWI' CURTIS.

"If you don't buy a----, at least buy a car made in the United Kingdom." That slogan was commonly seen in the British press before the war and it is one to which the potential car buyer in Britain after the war should give heed.

Irrespective of other factors, the Briton should buy British, not only to help maintain one of the country's most important industries and one that furnishes the third largest export value, but the British car is also the ideal vehicle for the average British motorist.

Past articles in the "Flywheel" have referred to outstanding technical developments on the Continent and to the advantages possessed by American cars over British in certain overseas markets, but none of these need concern the British family man requiring a family saloon for use in the U.K. The British manufacturers have developed models that fit the needs of the great bulk of local motorists and at prices within the reach of even slender purses.

Though British makers have long laboured under the disability of the horse-power tax they have still succeeded in building cars which will best meet the needs of the British motorist. At the same time revision of the horse-power tax may mean the development of types eminently suitable for overseas as well as local conditions — but that will not make the cars less desirable from the angle of the British buyer.

Strong efforts were made before the war by some American and Continental manufacturers to boost sales in Britain, but while they had some success the great bulk of cars sold were British. The high horse-power tax on the big motors restricted sales of American types to a small number of buyers whose particular requirements were such that excessive taxation was offset by some advantage. Turning to the continental makers, we find a number having distinctive (and to certain tastes,

very desirable) features, but in all but a very few cases such cars were far too expensive for the family motorist to consider. Those that compared in price with British cars generally suffered on comparison in certain other respects.

Conditions were somewhat different in the sports car field. There was no American sports car as the term is understood in Britain and Europe but there was a number of very fine European sports cars — at a very fine price! Enthusiasts dream of 'Bugs', Alfas, Delahayes, Delages, the B.M.W. and so on, but for all but the select few with bags of Bradburies, such cars will always be ephemeral. On the other hand, several British makers offered sports cars of definite merit at prices not much above those of family saloons, while the expensive British sports jobs were still cheaper than most of the European counterparts.

In the cheaper sports field the names of Morgan, M.G., S.S., H.R.G., and Riley occur as examples and it is hard to find foreign makes with comparable performance at anywhere near the same cost. In the steeper price bracket come makes such as Alta, Alvis, Aston-Martin, Bentley, Frazer-Nash, Lagonda — all having performance well in advance of mass-production standards and each distinguished by some feature or features setting it apart from the average sports car.

All in all, therefore, the Briton in search of a car giving all-round value-for-money need go no further than the home-produced product. It is designed to meet his needs and purse, it represents sound engineering practice and it is sound national economy for the nation to buy its national goods.

FLASH!! BEST FOR THE BRITON!

Blighty letter Nov. '44 states that a new car is being made, in Scotland post-war; 100,000 is first year's production figure. The price is to be under £100, and it is thought, by the letter correspondent, that a special projection engine will be used. The press gave full details, but unfortunately these were omitted... Our old friend 'Tom Thumb'?

MORRIS SERVICE STATION

by G. NOBLE.

All car owners at some time or another have seen the signs "Main Morris Agent" and "Authorised Morris Distributor" hung in front of repair stations, but have they ever stopped to think what lies behind this huge network of Morris Service covering the whole of the British Isles?

Contrary to expectations, these stations are in no way financed by Morris Motors but their association as regards service is as one. In every town of size there are main agents who are always in close rail and telephonic communication with Morris Motors and Morris technical advisers and representatives are constant visitors. These agents carry immense stocks of Morris spares and other makes of spares can be obtained during the same day if not in stock. The smaller agents around the district depend on the main agents and rely on them for accurate technical advice on methods of repair and modifications.

When the owner drives into the main service station he is met by a white-coated interviewer who will be interested to see that the owner receives the best results from his car, whether it be a Morris or otherwise. After the initial discussion of the nature of repair, the interviewer will consult the record system, where, surprising though it may seem, records of chassis and engine numbers, dates of sales, dates of previous repairs, changes of ownership, etc., are kept of most of the cars in that particular district. In this way, guarantee claims are facilitated and claims that are made on Morris Motors are rarely refused as the "Alma Mater" places implicit trust in the agent's decision.

When the owner leaves, with a definite promise of time for collection, the job passes to the mechanics who are skilled men and interested in their jobs. The repair finished, the car is tested by an employee whose only occupation is road testing. Thereafter he will report on any further defects in the car he may have noticed; they will be communicated to the owner on collection. If the owner wishes, an appointment can be made for these further repairs and the car collected and redelivered after the repairs have been carried out.

The agents have a day and night service and after an accident where loss of the car may mean a serious loss of business to the owner, a loan car can be supplied whilst awaiting the insurance company's decision.

This is a brief outline of the work carried on behind those little round signs, so remember, when you see at the foot of the agents' correspondence — "Ever at your Service" - it is genuine.

MORRIS SERVICE STATION

Fads & Fashions

BY P. C. HARRINGTON-JOHNSON

You might hear talk in the old 'local,' or the club 'natter,' of how little motorcycle design has changed since "the old days" or of how this or that promising design coming before its time, has been killed by the riding - buying public's conservatism. Yet all down. British motorcycle history there have been quaint outbursts of novelty-popular fads that raged for a while. Some of them stayed — good ideas that stood the test of time and have become standard practice. Others vanished with no trace save the junk yard or the used machine emporium.

War time, naturally, produces a crop of economy gadgets — extra-air or atomizing devices for carburation, 'spark intensifiers' and the like. Some of us recall those of 1914-20 followed by the post-last-war economy scooter craze.

Other queer fads that have been in their day, all the rage, include saddle tanks, the dirt track, grass track, competition pipes, nobbly tyres, George Dance knee grips, tank-top speedometers, auto-cycles, and now, perhaps, the second scooter craze.

Do you older riders remember the fashion

for carrying a spare inner tube in a leather drum round the handlebars — or the fad of fitting a leather tank-top tummy rest, bolted to the top tube? Saddle tanks largely killed that though the 'cam'. A.J.S. of the early '30's adapted the idea to saddle tanks very neatly. When A.J.S. triumphantly vindicated twist-grips in the 1925-27 I.O.M. races a crop of such grips came out — some failed to stay. Who now recalls the Bowden, the Dougherty or Douglas? From 1926 on, the "George Dance"-type John Bull-made racing knee-grips were absolutely essential on sports and racing mounts, yet today an entirely different riding position (and perhaps better road-holding) has made knee-grips just about unnecessary.

After the A.J.S. 1928 positive-stop foot-change in the T.T., a fad for these devices set in — Sturmey Archer being the first — with a standard conversion set. (Who remembers the Sunbeam four speed unit that would *never* work properly?) Another passing fad was a little lever bolting on to the clutch withdrawal lever, to give foot clutch control with hand **change**.

After much pioneering by Chater Lea with a beautifully neat design, saddle tanks, filling up unsightly corners and 'open spaces' in the frame, suddenly caught hold of popular fancy and in a year or so no machine was without one. They have stayed, but a similar idea that lasted only a season was the craze for overhead camshafts that bloomed-and faded — about 1926-29. Then there was the finned sump-cum-oil tank — all but universal around 1931....

Curiously enough, in these same years came three or four other- and passing-fads. One was, that 'the' machine was a 250 two-stroke (so every maker made one, for a year or two). Another was for 175 twostroke grass-track racers, and a dozen snappy models came out, almost all round the 172 Brooklands Villiers motor. Like the Ultra-Lightweight T.T. (175c.c.) the idea only lasted a couple of seasons. Yet another was jazz-painted saddle tanks — a very short-lived fad of 1929.

Slightly longer-lasting was the craze for putting speedos in the top of saddle tanks, and its sister fad for panelling the tank top with chromium strips in a decorative surround for the speedometer and tank caps. Some of the speedos were near the saddle nose and it is indeed a good thing *this* craze died speedily — the instruments were so hard to see on the road! A similar fad exists today for tank-top dash-panels — not altogether an unmixed blessing....

Who recalls nowadays the speedway craze of 1928-29, when almost every maker in England went dirt-track mad and cinder models were made even by such conservative firms as Scott,

Sunbeam, B.S.A., Norton, James Twin, Calthorpe, Triumph, Coventry Victor and Royal Enfield? Of the lot, Douglas was the most successful, but only the Rudge-Wallis-J.A.P. composite is found today.

B.S.A., in the Blue Star in 1931-32, set a trials craze and for several seasons upswept exhausts were the rule and a 'competition' specification a necessity. Yet one recalls the Enfield T.T. Racer of 1924, with just the same exhausts and a super specification, which would *not* sell till downswept pipes had been fitted....!

Chromeplating — after early troubles and some opposition (Yes,/ there was) has come to stay.

'Clean handlebars' and grouped controls, which enjoyed a big vogue from 1932-36, have largely faded out, as has the urge to fit all sports models with finned brakedrums and that other craze for hand-operated extra-oil pumps, usually feeding the cylinder barrel.

Just latterly there has been an urge to 148 o.h.v. engines — every popular make had to list one — just as about 1932 every popular make had at least one coil-ignition model. Two port exhausts was another craze which is still dying hard. The 98 c.c. utility machine was another fad which has faded — the sports 125 "flat-top" piston has superseded it.

Hints & Tips

A good scheme for any bike, but especially to a 'scrambler' or trials rider who may have falls, is to replace the metal front number plate with a sheet of ¼" thick leather, numbers being painted on, white on a black ground. Incidentally, this causes much less serious injuries to anyone in the event of a collision.

A tip for riders with shallow pockets — most of us, I think! When parking the machine see that the petrol tap is turned off, also ensure that it doesn't leak — so many do and several gallons are lost yearly for want of a tap washer replacement.

W hen on a regular run a good petrol saving dodge is to turn off the petrol when about 200 yards from the journey's end. The actual distance will vary with the size and appetite of the machine; these small quantities do mount up over a period of time. The above hint is particularly valuable to two-stroke riders using petroil. By shutting off early they avoid a sediment of pure oil in the mixing chamber, left after the petrol has evaporated, thus avoiding a gummed up jet or oiled plug when restarting the machine.

Do You Know?

That Sunbeams made a twin? It was an 8 h.p. J.A.P.- engined s.v. flat-tank, made for de-luxe side-car work between 1919 - 1922.

That Sunbeams also made a twostroke? This was the Seagull outboard motor, about 200 - 300 c.c. (water-cooled, of course) on the British market about 1934 - 1938.

That Rudges also marketed a twin? It was a 998 c.c. o.h.i.v. — very roughly, two Rudge Multi 500's on one V-crankcase. Timing gear was all-gear-drive, but the transmission, curiously enough, was by the first 3-speed Rudge gearbox — though the rest of the range (499 c.c. and 750 c.c. o.h.i.v. singles — yes, we've ridden 'em!) had the 20 speed multi (expanding pulley and metal plate clutch) gear and belt drive.

That Scotts have appeared in all three elements — land, (motorcycle and car) air. Flying Flea aircooled in-line twostroke inverted twin of 34 h.p. specially made for light plane use and costing £50-£60 — and water (an outboard water-cooled twin two-stroke of about 600 c.c. made between '30-'35.

Preparation (CONTD FROM P.11)

of all this work and what will the rider get out of it? The object, of course, is to get the best out of life and the reward — very little (in terms of £. S. D.) but what a thrill it will be when the boys come crowding round patting you on the back and saying, "I say, you old dodger, what have you been doing to that old scrap heap over the winter? I couldn't get near you down the straight." Yes, it's a glorious feeling to make the 'works' riders shaky. The only fly in the ointment is that old motors have been known to 'blow up' during the first day's racing. But, even so, the use of the file, hacksaw and drill continues unabated.

HIGHLAND Steed (CONTD. FROM P.12)

car in running order. I decided to sell, eventually getting £1. 10. 0. for the scrap; no, considering that I only paid £6. for the car to begin with, I really had quite a cheap six months running and can definitely say nothing but good in favour of the Jowett as a most reliable, cheap and easily maintained car. Indeed, there is only one fault — the second-hand price is extremely high, compared with other types, even up to 9 h.p..

CLUB NEWS

Time marches on! One may even say grows short and up to the time of going to press nothing has been done to form the M.M.C. competition teams, to take part in post-war trials, rallies, etc.. Old competition riders and would -be competitors are asked to give this matter a thought and if they are interested to hand in their names to any of the committee members, together with a few particulars as to experience, if any.

One does not have to be a super rider with a super machine to take part in a National Rally or main road trial and for very little outlay one is assured of an enjoyable weekend and maybe a 'pot' into the bargain.

It was very gratifying to see the grand 'turn-out' on March 5th. in 47·A's washouse, thus confirming the committee's decision to open up a 'large scale offensive.'

The Xmas number of the 'Flywheel' was ruined by somebody upsetting a brew of cocoa over it. Many scores of hours had been put into that number, and, it was produced in very cold weather, as you will remember, so please lads, a little more careful in future.

A s our time runs out and a breath of expectancy hangs over camp a short stocktaking will not be amiss. Those past few months in the 'cage' have been hard to bear, probably harder than any of our bad spells. It found most of the camp clubs — and they were legion, gradually fading away, through general apathy, cold, hunger and the hard to combat 'browned off' feeling.

M otoring seemed as remote as ever, with our forces still beyond the Zeigfried Line whilst on the other front the Oder remained a barrier; the cold was intense, overcrowding in the huts drove all to hopeless exasperation — in other words meetings ceased. We had maintained two club nights weekly for ten months, which in itself was a camp record, but we still carried on production of the "Flywheel". It is appropriate at this point to accord the appreciation which is due to the two 'full-time' members of the production staff. So, Bill Stobbs and you, Tom Rodger, accept the thanks of not so diligent club members who, from the 'horizontal', read the product of your industry.

pace does not permit the written tokens which many others have earned, but perhaps the consolation gained in time and labour well expended will, in itself be sufficient

- STRAAH -

36.

ROVER

ANIMO ET FIDE

One of Britain's Fine Cars

When in the South CONSULT

SPARSHATTS of

SOUTHAMPTON & PORTSMOUTH

SALES & SERVICE   HEAVY VEHICLE MAINTENANCE SPECIALISTS

Main agents for **DENNIS & DODGE**

SUPREME

OK SUPREME MOTORS LTD

WARWICK ROAD - GREET - BIRMINGHAM 11

MORRIS

ICH DIEN

BY APPOINTMENT

THE CAR WITH THE LOWEST UPKEEP COSTS

On August Bank Holiday the fourth of a series of discussions on The Ideal Car took place, and when the discussion closed it was quite easy to imagine the car that the majority of the M.M.C. considered "Ideal".

When the discussion opened some weeks ago it was pointed out that the car must be "Ideal" and not Utopian. "The Ideal" said Arthur Pill, introducing the subject, "is to produce a car that can be put on the market for £250 or less and that can be easily and cheaply maintained and is, therefore, a workable proposition." Maurice Airey followed up by giving a very interesting talk on the "Ideal" as he saw it, which must be a car that would be ownable, and would not look "dowdy" among even the most expensive cars. He pointed out that stream-lining not only gave the car "lines" but it gave a decidedly better performance, since it had been proved, in tests, that a streamlined car needed considerably less power to cover any distance in a given time than did a normal type of vehicle. Maurice was also in favour of a 'back-bone' chassis.

Allan Vidow, who was a motor mechanic in in civvy street, thought that a streamlined car looks very nice, but he considered that it should not be necessary to suspend a mechanic, feet uppermost—and then lower him down, head first into the bonnet which is almost necessary to carry out maintainance on some cars now. No, Allan wanted "Accessibility", and, therefore, lower maintainance costs.

It was finally decided, by an overwhelming majority, that the body should be a convertible coupé (capable of seating five persons) of the 2-door variety. The power unit, for which 70% of the designers voted was a 12 h.p. 4-cylinder model fitted with high camshafts similar to the Riley type. There was a good deal of discussion before this size was agreed to. Sizes suggested varied from 500 c.c.s to 30 h.p. (R.A.C. rating). The final decision was arrived at after it had been suggested (and later unanimously agreed to) that we should fit the motor with a turbo-supercharger, driven by exhaust gas, which would provide us with a boost of some 4/5 lbs. per sq. inch, and therefore give as much power as a larger engine with no increase in tax.

This engine in the opinion of the great majority of motorists present (America, Canada, Australia, South Africa and the U.K. were represented) should be mounted in an under slung chassis of the type we all know. Oleo suspension, independent at the front, was agreed to, although if a debated recount had been allowed it is quite possible that torsion-bar springing would have won the day.

The hydraulic braking system fitted to the modern car was considered satisfactory, and adopted but it was decided that a "hill-holder" brake, which allows the right foot to be used solely for acceleration (on hills) should be fitted. Further details regarding braking were not discussed, as it was pointed out that the war would be ending any year now and the club desired to finish the car.

The pre-war type of wheel was very popular with members but everyone wanted a different type of filling and finally knock-on Rudge hubs were agreed to. A low pressure tyre of 6" section was wanted by most although S. Roberts who introduced some very interesting points was in favour of a larger section, say 7.5".

Allan Bowman, who knows the American cars up to '42 as a Detroit designer, pointed out that many of the things that we consider refinements had already been fitted to low-price American cars built in 1940-1941. There is a gradual tendency, he explained, to keep the car of almost uniform width and shape from stem to stern. This gives the designer more scope to produce a body that looks well and is really big. The wings are no longer an "attachment" but a part of the car body and the line of the front wing goes straight back to the rear wheel. A rather unusual feature of our car is that we have the additional seat at the front owing to the fact that the body is wider here than where the rear seats are situated, between the back wheel arches. The left 2/3rds of the front seat folds back as an occasional bed.

The attached illustrations will give an idea as to what the finished car will look like — but do not be misled by the apparent overall length, the car would be some seventeenft. and is therefore almost identical with that of the average British "12".

America, it must be remembered continued to introduce new models long after British firms had switched over to war work. If we are to capture our share of the foreign markets we must advance our cars five years at one go. — hence --- "The Ideal Car."

Tom Swallow.

THE IDEAL CAR

Designed by MÜHLBERG MOTOR CLUB

SPECIFICATION

- **Engine:** R.A.C. rating 12.h.p. 4 cylinders, O.H.V. operated by push rods from two high-camshafts, low-pressure compressor giving boost of approx, 5lbs. per sq in. single dry-plate clutch.

- **Gearbox:** Synchromesh in unit construction with engine and clutch giving 4 forward speeds and reverse. Gear lever mounted on steering column.

- **Chassis:** Channel section with cross members, underslung. Suspension by enclosed helical springs, independent at front. Hydraulic shock absorbers. Lockheed hydraulic brakes. Drive taken to Hypoid rear axle by propellor shaft with Hardy-Spicer needle-bearing universals. Petrol tank mounted at rear.

- **Controls:** Telescopic spring-spoked steering wheel. Bishop cam-type steering box. Pistol-grip type hand brake lever fitted under facia panel on right hand side. Organ type accelerator pedal. Clutch foot-rest.

- **Carburettor:** Downdraught carburettor, fed by mechanical petrol pump.

- **Ignition:** By coil.
- **Lighting:** 12 volt electrical system. Sealed beam headlamps. Twin rear lights incorporating stop and reversing lamps. Ignition lock on steering column.

- **Wheels and Tyres:** Pressed-steel wheels carrying low pressure tyres of 6" section.

- **Body:** Fully streamlined two door convertible coupé giving ample accomodation for five adults, divided bench-type front seat seating three, rear seat holding two. The exterior presents a clean, rounded, well balanced appearance combining beauty of line with practical aerodynamic form. The two doors are of generous proportions, hinged at front in interests of safety and ease of entry and exit, the handles being recessed. Draughtless ventilation is provided for by small windows at front of each door. Opening from the top, the lid of the rear boot discloses roomy accomodation for luggage under which is a separate compartment housing spare wheel. Interior is designed to give maximum comfort. Seats have 'Dunlopillo' cushions and leather upholstery. Hypoid rear axle gives only shallow propellor shaft permitting abundant leg room for rear passengers. An interior light fitted to the rear of the front seat is provided. The driver's interests are looked after by narrow screen pillars giving good forward and side vision whilst the seat is fully adjustable both vertically and horizontally. The instruments are grouped in front of the driver, on the left of the dash is a glove compartment whilst the centre has provision for radio. Starter button is on dash, and there are locks to both doors. A full kit of tools is housed under the bonnet, which opens from the front in alligator fashion, giving easy access to the engine and facilitating routine maintainance attentions. Quick-fitting jacks for side of car are used and bumper bars are provided front and rear.

Maurice Airey

INTERESTED?

Interested motoring enthusiasts please note that two club meetings are held weekly. The Recce Hut on Sundays and Fridays will provide an interesting and informative evening. Two additional evening meetings are held weekly when trials, tuning and repair discussions etc., take place. For full club details see—

TOM SWALLOW, (Pres) 53.b.
ARTHUR PILL, (V-Chairm.) 47a.

*The endpapers illustrate the British and American interpretation of our **Ideal Car**.*